"A saucy combination of romance and suspense that is simply irresistible."
- Chicago Tribune

"Stylish... nonstop action...guaranteed to keep chick lit and mystery fans happy!"
- Publishers' Weekly, starred review

"Smart, funny and snappy... the perfect beach read!"
- Fresh Fiction

"If you have not read these books, then you are really missing out on a fantastic experience, chock full of nailbiting adventure, plenty of hi-jinks, and hot, sizzling romance. Can it get any better than that?"
- Romance Reviews Today

"(A) breezy, fast-paced style, interesting characters and story meant for the keeper shelf. 4 ½!"
- RT Book Reviews

# OTHER BOOKS BY GEMMA HALLIDAY

# OTHER BOOKS BY T. SUE VERSTEEG

# LUCK BE A LADY

---

a Tahoe Tessie mystery

## GEMMA HALLIDAY
### &
## T. SUE VERSTEEG

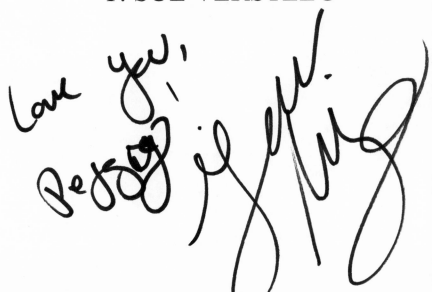

This book is dedicated to my dad and mom, Clark and Kathy VerSteeg. Thanks for always being there, no matter what. I love you both. And, since release day falls on your special day, Happy Birthday, Mom!

Also, a few words of thanks. First and foremost, thank you, God! Jeremiah 29:11

Gemma, thank you for this fabulous opportunity, the chance to help breathe life into Tessie and her entourage. I find it odd to say this as a writer, but words just aren't enough. You are in for a huge hug one day. Start preparing now.

All of the people at Ozarks Romance Authors, I'm so proud to be part of such a talented group of writers.

Ursula Gorman, Trula Wyatt, Trisha Kiefer, Cassandra Curtis, and Casey Nichols, thank you so much for always being there to critique, beta read, encourage, or whatever I need. You are fabulous.

And, last but certainly not least, thank you, Super Hubby! My Stephen, you've been a rock and cattle prod (Not at the same time…usually) through my entire writing career. I love and adore you.

~ T. Sue

A huge thank you to all of the people who helped make this book shine, including Susan Thompson, Michelle Seeds, Tim Stout, Lyndsey Lewellen, Jackson Stein, and, last but never least, T. Sue VerSteeg. You crack me up, girl.

~Gemma

# CHAPTER ONE

———

When I was ten, my dad taught me how to play blackjack. I'd proudly shown him my fourth grade report card bearing the A I'd earned in math, and he'd said, "Nice work, Tessie. Now let's put those skills to good use." He'd taken me upstairs to the VIP blackjack tables in the back of his casino, set me up with one of his dealers in a crisp, white shirt, and taught me the art of counting to twenty-one. I heard him bragging later to his director of operations what a quick study I was. In two hours, I'd cleaned him out of $600 in chips.

That was almost twenty years ago, but it was still one of my most vivid memories of him. Though, to be honest, I didn't have a whole lot of memories of my father to choose from. Mom and he split when I was just two, and she'd promptly moved me south to Berkeley and away from the high-rolling life my father had carved out for himself here. I'd grown up only seeing him every other Christmas and during summer breaks. Our relationship wasn't what you'd call close, but it wasn't strained either. I guess I'd always looked at Richard King more like one would a fun uncle than a father figure.

Which is why I was surprised at how hard it was to keep tears from running down my face as they lowered his casket into the ground. I sniffed, my nose starting to run as much from the cold as the grief, as I tried to look anywhere but at the polished mahogany surface in front of me.

Across the grass, still spotted with melting snow, stood my father's widow, Britton. Britton was blonde, thanks to her stylist, busty, thanks to her plastic surgeon, and at least twenty years my dad's junior. She was dressed in all black, a skin-tight Donna Karen dress underneath a faux fur that engulfed her petite frame like a giant gorilla suit. While I enjoyed my designer shoes as much as the next girl, Britton took the notion of fashion to a whole new level. One that was bedazzled, bling-ed, and bleached within an inch of its life.

Beside Britton stood Alfonso Malone, or Alfie, my father's Director of Operations and head of security. Tall, grim, and not someone I'd want to meet in a dark alley. A scar ran across his cheek, his nose lay at a crooked angle, and his voice held a deep gravel that spoke of a hard life before donning the expensive suits he wore to be my dad's right-hand man. He had a comforting arm around Britton, but his eyes were firmly fixed on the casket, almost as if he was examining it for proof my dad was really in there.

Surrounding them was a slew of people dressed in black who I didn't know. Not surprising, considering it had been some time since I'd seen my father. A year? Two? I couldn't remember now. To be honest, the allure of the blackjack tables had long ago faded for me. While I'd inherited my father's blue eyes and strawberry blonde hair—leaning just a little more to the strawberry than blonde—he'd failed to pass on his love of high-stakes games. Especially ones that favored the house.

I shifted, my feet going numb from the cold in my black pumps as the priest said his final words over the casket. Mourners began to disperse, nodding sympathetically in my direction, patting Britton on the shoulder, awkwardly shuffling back to their cars in their overcoats and boots, trying not to slip on the icy mud.

In the winter, Tahoe was a magical wonderland, the pristine snow on the evergreens and jagged mountains brilliant enough to take your breath away. In the spring, the snow melted to reveal enough mud puddles to make a kindergartener squeal with delight. This was March, and the town was just starting to lose its magical sheen.

"Hey, Tessie," I heard a deep voice say behind me.

Even before I spun around to face him, I knew who it belonged to. Rafe Lorenzo. Pro snowboarder, sponsored by my father's casino, minor local celebrity, and my first crush.

"Rafe," I said, turning away from the casket to face him.

"I'm so sorry, Tess," he said, emotion etched on his face.

I nodded. "Thank you," I responded, trying to adjust my eyes to the adult version of the first boy I'd ever doodled my name in hearts with.

When I was a teenager, Rafe had been in his early twenties, just coming into his own on the mountain, and charming enough that my father had threatened to take out his knees if he ever so much as held my hand. Not that the threat had kept me from fantasizing about just that. The same daredevil charm and charisma that had made him such a lucrative ambassador for my father's resort also made for a dangerous temptation to a girl whose adolescent hormones were running amuck.

While Rafe still wore his dark hair a little too long, letting it curl at the ends around his neck, his face was leaner and more angular now than it had been. A few faint laugh lines tickled the corners of his eyes, but his skin was the same warm, Mediterranean tan I'd remembered. And his eyes, staring at me now with genuine concern, were the same brilliant green and rimmed in long, black lashes that I'd gotten lost in as a teenage romantic.

I strongly reminded myself what good practice I'd had at keeping my hormones in check since then.

"You look great, Tess," Rafe observed. "You haven't changed a bit."

My cheeks heated despite the biting wind. "Thanks," I mumbled. "You too."

"Bullshit. I totally look ten years older," he replied, though the corners of his mouth turned up, deepening those laugh lines at his eyes.

I felt a small grin pulling my lips in response. It felt good. I realized it might have been the first time in days that I'd smiled. "Has it really been ten years?"

"At least. Last time I saw you, you were heading off to art school, planning to make your mark as the next great American painter."

"That was a long time ago," I agreed, feeling the smile drop from my face. "I curate now. A small gallery in San Francisco. Mission Arts."

"Don't tell me you've given up painting?"

I shrugged. "Turns out being a starving artist isn't actually as glamorous as I thought."

He chuckled, the sound warm, rumbling, and totally incongruent with our grim surroundings. "Well, I'll have to check out your gallery next time I'm in The City."

The fact that we both knew it was a hollow threat pulled an awkward pause over the conversation. I shifted in my pumps again. Rafe ran a hand through his thick hair.

Finally Rafe broke the tension by asking, "So how are you doing? You okay?"

I nodded, stealing a glance at the casket again. "I will be," I replied by rote. I'd fielded this same question at least a dozen times since getting the news via Britton's text message that my father had suddenly passed away. The past two days had been a blur of last-minute travel arrangements and subdued murmurs of sympathy from strangers. Or, in Rafe's case, resurrections from my past.

Rafe shook his head, his hair skimming the collar of his wool coat turned up against the cold. "Heart attack," he said, eyes cutting to the closed casket, too. "Who would have thought any part of Richard King was weak, let alone his heart?"

I nodded in agreement. Shot execution style, I might have expected in his line of work. Possibly dumped in the frigid waters of Lake Tahoe. But my father succumbing to something as mundane as a heart attack? I could almost hear him rolling over in his freshly-dug grave at the thought.

"You coming back to the casino?" Rafe asked. "Britton's hosting a wake of sorts in the penthouse."

"Oh, I, uh, I'm not sure..." I trailed off. I watched Britton get into a town car, the other guests filing into their vehicles. Honestly, the last thing I wanted to do was replay the same awkward sentiments of sympathy with a roomful of people who all knew my father better than I did. What I wanted to do was go back to my rental car, crank up the heater, and listen to old Sinatra songs—my dad's favorite—as I made the drive over the hill and home to San Francisco.

He must have sensed my hesitation, as Rafe put a hand on my arm. "He loved you, Tessie."

This admission took me by surprise. "I, um, I loved him, too," I said, the words sticking in my throat, causing those tears to back up again.

"Come back to the casino, Tessie." He paused. "At least to say good-bye."

Put like that, how could I refuse?

* * *

The Royal Palace Casino and Resort was located on the border of South Lake Tahoe, California and Stateline, Nevada. And when I say "on the border," I mean the state line ran the entire length of the parking lot. One inch over the Nevada border, Dad had erected the first line of slot machines on casino property.

South Lake Tahoe was primarily a tourist town, playing host to Silicon Valley execs and wealthy entrepreneurs on their three-day weekends. The locals were die-hard skiers and snowboarders whose jobs largely centered around the tourists, a small trade-off for living in the winter sports paradise. The landscape was dotted with million-dollar ski chalets mingling with weather-worn cottages and old motels converted into apartments. Ski bums and nature lovers who worshiped the mountains mixed with weekenders who worshiped the casinos, spas, and souvenir boutiques lining Lake Tahoe Boulevard.

And in the center of it all sat the lake itself, almost two-hundred square miles of crystal blue waters. My father named me after the legendary "Tahoe Tessie" monster that was supposedly the local version of its more famous Loch Ness cousin. Not that I really believed in that kind of folklore. And, trust me, my father hadn't been the fanciful type either. But he knew a publicity opportunity when he saw it. Any chance to draw more tourists to the Royal Palace's slots, that man was all over it. Even when it came to naming his only child.

Next door to the Royal Palace sat Harrah's casino, and just across the street were their two competitors, Harvey's and the Deep Blue. And just over the border on the California side sat a handful of boutiques, restaurants, and ski equipment rental shops, soaking in the casinos' tourist overflow.

I pulled up to the front of the Royal Palace. It was eighteen stories of neon-rimmed glass and steel. The main gambling floors sat in front, windowless chambers with flashing signs advertising showgirls, magicians, and the latest aging rock band booked into the amphitheater behind the parking structure. Flanking the main building were the turret style towers, holding guest rooms. They jutted into the bright blue sky, breaking up the scenery of pine trees and snow dusted peaks with giant billboards at their apex, letting everyone know that the buffet was only $4.99 on Wednesdays.

While there was no other word but "gaudy" to describe the building, it had an almost predictably commercial charm about it that was oddly comforting.

I left my car with a valet sporting dark hair and lots of freckles and entered the lobby. Here the gaudy goodness was even more prevalent, my father having delighted in being the "King" of his "Royal" palace. He'd embedded touches of his theme everywhere, from the "Princess Day Spa" on the second floor, to the "King's Court All You Can Eat Buffet" located in the west wing of the building. In the lobby, the floors were polished marble leading to the check-in desk, lined in gold and dotted with fake family crests. The gaming floor dinged with a thousand slot machines all going at once, and the air held a thick haze of cigarette smoke, indoor smoking being legal on this side of the border. It was a scent I should have hated, but it instantly brought me back to my childhood, dragging with it bittersweet memories that threatened those tears again.

I swallowed down the lump in my throat as I hit the east bank of elevators, stepped into an empty carriage, and keyed in my code for the penthouse.

"Ohmigod, Tessie, I'm so glad you came!" The second I walked into the penthouse suite, Britton attacked me with air kisses.

"Hi, Britton," I said, extracting myself from an embrace that smelled like peaches and Chanel No. 5. I scanned the room behind her for a glimpse of Rafe's tall frame, but the room was a sea of people in black who all blended together.

"When did you get in?" Britton asked, twirling her hair with one hand, holding a martini with the other.

"Just a couple of hours ago," I answered, craning around her to see where she'd gotten the drink from. I could definitely use one.

"Well, we'll totally have to catch up. Lunch tomorrow?"

I shifted my feet. "Actually, I'm not staying."

"What do you mean you're not staying?"

"I...have to get back to work." Which was true. While the owner of Mission Arts had told me to take as much time as I needed, we had a show this weekend. I was already starting to get antsy about leaving my artists in someone else's hands.

"Oh. Right. Work," Britton said, wrinkling her nose up at the four letter word.

She sipped at her drink, letting her eyes wander around the room, an uncomfortable silence falling between us. I'd only met Britton a couple of times. In fact, since leaving for college, I'd only been to Tahoe a couple of times. Work, life, and schedules had gotten in the way. Two-and-a-half years, I decided as I stood there, coveting Britton's drink. That's how long it had been since I'd stepped foot in the penthouse. Not that anything had changed. The walls were still covered in the same flocked, fleur-de-lis wallpaper and spotted with museum-quality paintings. Imported Persian rugs covered polished hardwood, the chandeliers dripping from the ceiling with crystals from the Liberace collection. The penthouse was exactly the same, the casino exactly the same. Even Britton was the same. With possibly the exception of her lips, which seemed a little fuller.

"I had them done."

"What?" I asked, blinking at her.

"My lips. I saw you staring at them. I had them done. Restylane."

"Oh, I, uh…"

"It's awesome. Lasts for like six months without a follow up. You should totally try it."

I wasn't sure if I'd just been insulted or if this was Britton's brand of small talk.

But before I had a chance to respond she completely changed gears. "God, it's not going to be the same without him around here," she said, taking a generous gulp of her martini.

"He was a presence, wasn't he?" I agreed.

Britton sniffed loudly. "It was just so sudden, you know?" she said, cocking her head at me. "One minute totally lively, the next, like, gone."

I felt that odd lump in the back of my throat again and squashed it down. "Was he sick?" I asked.

She shook her head. "No. I mean he was, like, totally healthy. Energetic, strong, virile as hell…"

"Okay, that's enough." The last thing I wanted to hear about was my dead father's virility.

Britton teared up. "I'm just gonna miss him so much, Tessie."

And then she hugged me. Not a dainty air-kiss thing, but a full-bodied hug that threatened to spill vodka down the back of my little black dress.

I awkwardly put my arms around her shoulders, patting her back. I glanced around the room, trying to catch someone's eye for help.

Unfortunately, the eye I caught was dark, beady, and belonged to someone I recognized only too well. Buddy Weston, owner of the Deep Blue casino across the street. He was short, stocky, and wore a gaudy, teal silk shirt and matching tie beneath his blazer, both of which shimmered under the chandelier's lighting.

"Ladies," he said, approaching us.

At the sound of his voice, Britton detached herself and turned around to face him. Immediately her eyes went from tearful to suspicious, narrowing beneath her false lashes as her jaw tensed. "What the hell are you doing here, Weston?"

He raised an eyebrow at her, one big, bushy thing. "I came to pay my respects. Dick and I had our business differences, but we were peers of a sort."

"Ha!" Britton blasted out. Loudly enough that I wondered just how many martinis she'd had since returning from the cemetery. "You tried to shut Dick down every chance you got."

"Business. Nothing personal."

"Easy to say now that he's gone," she shot back.

Weston smiled tightly, a benign thing that didn't quite reach his beady eyes. "I guess we're all in a better financial place now that he is, aren't we, Britton?"

Her eyes narrowed so far they were just tiny slits, her brows pulling down into angry slashes. "Exactly what are you implying, Weston?"

"Nothing. Nothing at all." Buddy cut his eyes to a painting on the wall. "Is that a Vermeer? Lovely. Priceless. Yours now, no?"

"Get out!" Britton shouted. Causing several heads to turn our way. "Get the hell out of our casino, and don't you dare come back."

Weston smiled his tight smile at Britton again, any emotion behind it completely unreadable. Then he turned to me, nodded, and made his way toward the exit.

Britton waited until the heavy double doors closed behind him before letting out a long sigh, declaring to the room in general, "God, I need another drink," and heading off toward the bar I'd yet to find.

"Hurricane Britton strikes again," a gravelly voice at my elbow observed. Alfie.

"In her defense, he's a jerk," I pointed out.

Alfie nodded. "That he is," he agreed. Then he turned to face me. "It's nice to see you, Tessie. I wish it were under better circumstances."

"Thank you," I answered, knowing that was as close to emotion as Alfie was likely to display.

"How long are you in town for?" he asked.

"Leaving tonight," I said, making the decision on the spot. I'd had enough of the Royal Palace.

Alfie frowned. "I had hoped you'd stay for a few days. I have an appointment set up for you with your father's attorney tomorrow."

"His attorney?" I asked. "Why?"

"To go over the terms of your father's will."

I bit my lip. While my father lived large, I had no idea what his actual net worth was. I guess I'd always figured most of what was in his penthouse belonged to the casino. He lived on site, drove company cars. It was a lifestyle, but I didn't know how much of it he actually owned. I couldn't keep my eyes from straying to the Vermeer hanging on the wall.

"I don't want anything," I heard myself say, almost meaning it. The painting was amazing, and I would have loved to give it a good home.

"It's not that simple," Alfie responded. Though something in the tightness of his voice made me think he wished it was.

"What do you mean?"

"I mean the pronoun Britton used just now to describe the casino wasn't entirely accurate." He paused. "When she told Weston to get out of *our* casino. It isn't ours or even hers."

He paused again, and I felt an odd ball of anxiety instantly grow in my gut, the words ringing in my ears even as he said them.

"It's *yours*. The casino now belongs to you, Tessie."

# CHAPTER TWO

———

"What do you mean it's mine?" I asked, feeling a frown burrow between my brows as I studied the man across the table from me the next day.

After Alfie's bombshell last night, I'd asked the exact same question of *him*. But all he'd tell me is that my father's attorney would discuss everything with me in the morning. I gave up, found the bar, ordered a very stiff drink, then reluctantly trudged downstairs to ask the clerk on duty at check-in for a room for the night. But apparently Alfie had already arranged *that*, too, and a suite was waiting for me. I'd tossed and turned all night in the thousand-thread-count sheets, wondering exactly what kind of mess my father was dragging me back into here.

And this morning I was finding out, as I faced my father's attorney, Stintner, and Alfie across a huge glass table in my father's conference room, papers filled with legalese littering the surface.

"You are your father's only child," Stintner explained to me.

"Yes. I'm aware."

"As such, the casino is yours."

I shook my head. "Doesn't the casino belong to shareholders or a parent company or something? It's not like grandma's silver that can just be handed to me."

"Of course." Stintner nodded. He had white hair, a slim frame, and a large nose and pair of Dumbo ears that seemed two sizes too big for his petite frame. "A shareholder conglomerate technically owns the Royal Palace. However, Mr. King was one of the largest shareholders and chairman of the board of directors that ran the casino. He named you as his successor."

"Successor?" I repeated, feeling that frown burrow deeper. "That can't be. Look, I run a gallery. Art, that's what I know."

"Your father seemed to think otherwise," Stintner told me. "Believe me, he had several candidates to choose from, but he was adamant about naming you."

I bit my lip, an odd mix of emotions rolling in my belly. The fact that my father had such faith in my abilities filled me with a warm sort of pride. At the same time, I knew that faith was totally misplaced. Sure, I'd been able to deal five-card draw, seven-stud, Texas hold'em, and high/low Chicago style poker all before I was old enough to drive. But that had been a long time ago. I hadn't even picked up a deck of cards in ages. And knowing how to play cards was a far cry from running a multi-million dollar a year resort.

I'd grown up living in Berkeley, the child of a single, working mother. While we'd always had enough to eat and a decent roof over our heads, my summers at the casino had been my only glimpse into the lifestyles of the rich and spendthrift. I wasn't too proud to admit that overseeing an organization of this size, dealing in the sort of numbers they did on a daily basis, was way over my head.

"Look," Stintner said, sensing my clear hesitation, "the fact is, like it or not, you are the chairman for the time being."

"For the time being," I said, jumping on the words.

The lawyer shot Alfie a look. "The board will obviously want to convene to discuss the future of the casino. At that time, if you so desire, you can withdraw as chairman and let the board appoint someone else."

Withdrawing sounded good. In fact, withdrawing *now* rather than waiting sounded even better.

"How about if I just resign now?" I asked. "How about I just go home and let you guys run the place until the board convenes, huh?"

Alfie's eyes narrowed. Stintner cleared his throat loudly.

"I'm afraid that's not a very good idea," he said. "Casino shares are likely to plummet when shareholders get wind of the fact we have no official chairman at the helm. Investors are nervous enough as it is, what with your father..." he trailed off.

"Dying," I supplied for him. "It's okay, I'm aware he's dead."

He cleared his throat loudly. "Yes, well. So are they. And they're not happy. The casino is in a very precarious situation right now."

My head was spinning trying to process all of this. "So, let me get this straight. If I wait until the board convenes and appoints a new chairman, the investors keep their cool, and everyone is happy. But if I go home now, the casino risks going under?"

Stintner nodded, his hair bobbing up and down. "Correct."

I took a deep breath, closing my eyes as I imagined my father making these arrangements with Stintner in the first place. My mother never made a secret of the fact she hated the casino business and the shady lifestyle that went along with it. As a kid, I'd thought it was kind of cool. No bedtimes, no boring homework, and lots of flash. As an adult, the novelty had worn off quickly, the flash on the outside revealing very little of substance on the inside. I'd immersed myself in the art scene instead, creating my own niche in the world that now had very little to do with neon lights and all-you-can-eat buffets.

Until now.

"When can the board convene?" I asked.

"Ten days," Stintner answered.

Ten days. That was the longest I'd spent at the Royal Palace since high school. I cringed, thinking of the mess I'd be going back to in my own life after ten days away. I'd miss the show. My artists would think I'd abandoned them. Plus, there was my cat. I had a sad vision of him using every piece of furniture I owned as a scratching post in protest of being alone for ten whole days.

But it was either abandon them, or my father's casino, his vision, his baby, and the hundreds of people who relied on it for their families.

"Fine," I said on a deep exhale. "Ten days. But that's it. I'm out as soon as the board meets."

Stintner visibly relaxed, the tension draining from his shoulders. Alfie was still expressionless.

"So, what do I have to do?" I asked them.

"Nothing," Alfie quickly cut in. "I'll run the day-to-day. You're just a figurehead. Like the queen. Just sit there and look official." He stood up, buttoning the top button on his blazer as he continued. "The board will convene on the ninth. Just try to stay out of trouble until then."

I couldn't help my eyes rolling back in my head. Seriously, it wasn't like I was that fifteen year-old trying to sneak up to the slots anymore.

But before I could clue Alfie in, he turned on his wingtips and marched out of the conference room, heading toward the elevators.

Fine. I could do figurehead. Just ten days, then I could go back to my real life and leave the Royal Palace in the world of memories where it belonged. Alfie's delivery might have been abrasive, but I planned to do exactly as he suggested. Stay out of trouble and ride out the ten days until I could go home.

To that aim, I knew the perfect place to start—the casino's spa.

* * *

I rode the elevators back down to my room and dialed down to the Princess Day Spa. I'd just gotten off the phone, confirming that they had an opening for a massage and pedi that afternoon, when a knock sounded at my door.

I peeked through the peephole, not able to disguise the groan that slipped from my lips when I saw Britton's bleached-blonde self staring back at me.

I briefly thought about not answering, but even as I entertained that thought, my cell buzzed to life on the nightstand, Britton's name coming up on the caller ID. I could run, but chances were I couldn't hide from her for ten whole days.

Reluctantly, I opened the door to find her tapping one designer heel against the carpet, pink cell in hand.

"Oh. Hey, I was just calling you. I thought maybe you were out."

"Nope," I answered. "Right here. What can I do for you, Britton?"

Which she took as an invitation to come in, flopping herself down on my double bed. "I need your help," she sighed. "We have an issue with one of the VIP guests."

I frowned. "*My* help?"

"Yeah. Ellie said you're in charge now?"

"Who's Ellie?"

"Penthouse housekeeping. She heard it from Buckie, the valet, who heard it from Tate at the front desk, who overheard Alfie telling Dave in security to keep an eye on you in the surveillance booth."

Mental face palm. I looked up at the ceiling, half expecting Alfie to have wired my room with cameras, too.

"So, it's true, right?" Britton pressed. "Ellie almost never gets a rumor wrong. Dickie left you in charge?"

I paused before answering, suddenly wondering what my father had left Britton in his will. The lifestyle she'd enjoyed had come with the position of chairman's wife. Once the board appointed a new one, would Britton be ousted?

Suddenly I sort of felt sorry for Britton. But if she was worried, it didn't show in her heavily-lined eyes, wide in anticipation of my answer.

"Sort of," I mumbled. "Only technically."

But that was good enough for Britton. "Fab. So, here are the deets: one of the guests just called to the front desk saying stuff was missing from his room. You need to go check it out."

"Isn't this the kind of thing we have security for?" I protested.

Britton nodded. "Yes, but the guests like a personal touch. Dickie always did that stuff himself. He said it smoothed feathers and loosened wallets faster."

I'll bet.

I glanced at the clock. I had two hours before my scheduled massage. "Okay, fine. I guess I could go try to smooth some feathers."

"Cool! Let's go," Britton said, popping up off my bed.

"Did you always come with my dad?" I asked as she led the way down the corridor to the bank of elevators.

Britton shook her head. "No, but I figure you're a rookie. You might need some back-up."

I looked down at her outfit. Britton was dressed in gold stilettos, a pink mini dress, and about a dozen silver bangles. If this was my back-up, God help me.

One elevator ride later we were on the tenth floor of the east turret tower. This was the wing where the hotel's whales, their high rollers, stayed. The hope was the luxury accommodations would keep them on the gambling floor and not out on the ski slopes. Usually it worked, too.

Outside the door to room 1012 a guy in a black "security" jacket stood guard.

"Hey, Johnny," Britton said, waving at him.

He nodded. "Mrs. King." He looked at me and did a duplicate of the nod. "Ms. King."

I'd never met the guy before, so I could only deduce that Johnny was on the same rumor circuit as the penthouse housekeeping staff.

Either that or he'd already been watching me on Alfie's monitors.

"Mr. Carvell inside?" Britton asked the guy.

He nodded again. "Oh yeah. Not too happy, either."

"No worries. That's why Tessie's here," Britton said, giving me a huge smile.

I bit my lip. She had a whole lot more faith in my ability to smooth feathers than I did.

Johnny opened the door to the suite for us, and Britton and I walked inside.

The room took up roughly the space of four normal guest rooms, a sunken living room in the center, a kitchenette and wet bar to the right, and a doorway leading to a bed and bath on the left. The floors were hardwood covered in soft rugs, the furnishings modern and sleek, and the windows covering the back wall displayed a view of the snow-covered Sierras that rivaled any artwork the hotel's designer could have hung.

Along the wall near the wet bar sat a large, mahogany armoire. Alfie, another guy in a black security jacket, and a man with thinning hair and acne scars wearing an expensively tailored suit stood next to the open cabinet.

Alfie looked up when we entered, his eye twitching ever so slightly at the sight of me. I squelched the urge to tell him the feeling was mutual.

"Mr. Carvell, I am so sorry this happened," Britton gushed, surging forward with her signature air kisses. "But rest assured we will get to the bottom of it. This," she said, beaming, "is Dick's daughter, Tessie. She's running the casino now."

"Uh, temporarily," I mumbled, sticking a hand out to shake Carvell's.

He nodded at me. "Pleased to meet you."

"Likewise," I told him. "I'm sorry it's under such unpleasant circumstances. Is there anything I can do?"

"Security is handling it," Alfie quickly cut in.

I paused, thought 'smoothing' thoughts, and pulled out my biggest smile. "Glad to hear it. I know they're very capable."

"I hope so," Carvell said. "I can't afford a loss like this." He paused. "And I wouldn't expect it at the Royal Palace," he added, the meaning behind it clear: fix this or I'm playing somewhere else.

"Understood," Alfie assured him. "So, you said you put your cash in the safe?"

Carvell nodded, gesturing to the mahogany chest. "Yes. In there. About midnight."

Up close I could tell that it wasn't just a decorative piece of furniture. A black, metal safe sat inside one of the cupboards.

"How much cash?" I asked.

Alfie shot me a look, clearly willing me to be a *silent* figurehead.

"Five grand."

I couldn't help the small whistle that escaped me at the amount.

"Is there a reason you had such a large sum of cash in your room, Mr. Carvell?" Alfie asked.

The guy pursed his thin lips together, looked down at the carpet, shuffled his feet a bit.

"Mr. Carvell?" Alfie prompted again.

"All right. I was invited to a high-stakes poker game later tonight. This was the buy-in."

Alfie's eye twitched again. While it was impossible to police, casino staff did not look kindly on side games in their hotel. If they didn't get a piece of the action, it generally wasn't allowed.

But, considering the circumstance, Alfie glossed over the admission, asking instead, "Did you know the person who invited you?"

"Not really. I met him at the tables downstairs yesterday morning."

Alfie and the security guy shared a look. My radar perked up. Clearly this tidbit of info meant something to them.

"Was he a guest, too?" I asked.

Alfie narrowed his eyes at me. I did a silent "what?" shrug in his direction.

"I don't know. I assumed so," Carvell answered.

"Did you happen to get a name?" Alfie asked.

"Price. The guy said his name was Price, and that I should meet him in room 1424 at ten tonight." Carvell looked from Alfie to the security guy. "Why? You think this Price guy had something to do with it?"

"What time did you notice the cash missing?" the security guy asked, avoiding the question, I noticed.

"Just now. I called down right away."

"Has anyone else been in your suite with you?" I asked.

Alfie sent me a snarl to go with his narrowed eyes. Geeze, he was territorial. I rolled my own pair of baby-blues, then did a zipping-the-mouth-and-locking-it-shut thing.

"No," Carvell answered. "It's just been me."

"Between midnight when you deposited the cash and just now when you noticed it missing, how long were you out of your suite?" Alfie asked.

Carvell chewed his lower lip, thinking. "A couple hours, maybe. I went to bed right after I locked up the money. But I had breakfast in the café downstairs this morning, then might have stopped to play a hand or two at the tables."

"And you're sure the door was locked when you left?"

Carvell nodded vigorously. "Completely sure."

I glanced back at the door we'd just come through. Like the rest of the suite, it was in pristine condition. The fact that the lock wasn't broken was a clear sign we were looking at an inside job of some sort. Card key codes were wiped and recoded every time a customer checked out. Unless someone had swiped Carvell's key, stolen his cash, then returned said key to his possession, all without him knowing, whoever had entered the room had to have a master key.

Alfie must have come to the same conclusion I did, as his eyes went dark, the line of his mouth tightening. I suddenly felt a little sorry for the thief. I shuddered to think what Alfie would do to an employee caught stealing.

"Look, can't you guys just take a look at your security tapes?" Carvell said. "You got cameras all over the place. Just look at who was leaving my room this morning."

Alfie and his security shared that look again.

"Actually," the security guy said, "we don't use tape anymore. It's all digitized and logged by computers."

"So check the damned computer then," Carvell told him, his voice rising in proportion to his obvious frustration.

Alfie cleared his throat. "I wish we could. Our system experienced some turbulence this morning resulting in gaps in our currently available footage."

I raised an eyebrow at Alfie. While his language was vague enough, the meaning was alarming. "Are you saying someone messed with your system in order to erase the theft?"

His eyes shot to mine, clearly thinking a whole list of dirty words.

"Our techs are working on recovering the footage," his security guy answered.

"Oh, that's just great!" Carvell said, throwing his arms up.

"Was anything else taken?" Alfie asked, trying to pull Carvell's attention away from the security team's apparent inadequacies. "Any personal items?"

Carvell shook his head. "Not that I noticed. I didn't do a full inventory before I called you guys, but I travel fairly light. Do you need me to do that now?"

"Please," Alfie said.

Carvell sighed deeply, then moved into the bedroom. "Okay, let's go look."

Alfie and the security guy followed him, leaving Britton and me alone.

"Carvell's one of our high rollers," Britton confided in me as soon as he left the room.

"Oh?" I asked, wandering over to the armoire to get a closer look at the safe.

"He sells cars," she explained. "He owns six dealerships in the Bay Area. Comes up here a couple times a month to blow a wad when sales are up." She paused. "Or when his wife is getting on his nerves."

"Has he ever played in private games here before?"

"Not that I know of," Britton told me. "But it's not something he'd advertise, right?"

"Good point," I agreed.

I peered into the cabinet at the now empty black box. I didn't know a lot about safes myself, not actually owning anything worth locking away, but it looked fairly standard. Much like the one we used at the gallery to house our pricier pieces before a show. Only this one was smaller, the interior shoebox sized, and made of thick, fire-safe metal. The door had a keypad on it with several numbers and a little screen. Neither looked damaged. Whoever had broken into the safe hadn't used force. While it didn't look like Fort Knox, it clearly took someone who knew what they were doing more than I did to get into it.

A master key, a knowledge of safe cracking, and the ability to take out the casino's security footage. Not only were we looking at an insider, but I had a bad feeling we were also looking at a pro.

# CHAPTER THREE

———

As soon as Alfie and his security guy ascertained that the cash was the only thing missing, we all left Carvell and dispersed at the elevators. Alfie and his sidekicks took the service elevator to the control room, while Britton headed up to the penthouse, saying she had someone coming in to help her pack up my dad's things.

I tried to ignore how final that sounded. Instead, I looked down at my watch. I still had an hour and a half before my spa appointment. I hit the lobby button on the elevator, riding it down to the main floor. I had a bad feeling I hadn't done all that much to smooth Mr. Carvell's feathers. Yet.

Four clerks were on duty at the check-in desk: a red-head with a pair of ruby lips, a brunette woman in her forties, a guy in a suit who had a "manager" tag pinned to his lapel, and a large, Hispanic guy with dyed blond hair humming a Bette Midler tune to himself. I made a bee-line for the blond.

He spotted me as I approached, throwing both hands up in the air and doing a squeal that could have come from a twelve-year-old girl. "Tessie King, as I live and breathe, is that you, darling?"

I couldn't help an answering grin. "Hi, Tate. It's great to see you," I told him truthfully, coming in for a hug over the top of the counter.

Tate was about my age, and his mother had worked at the Royal Palace for as long as I could remember. As kids, we'd spent countless lazy summer days by the pool together. As an adult, Tate hadn't wandered far, his love of the casino world only growing where mine had waned. But it hadn't kept me from enjoying my last summer before art school here with him, day-tripping to Reno for mall runs, and enjoying "girl days" at the spa.

"Baby, I am so sorry about your dad. Are you doing okay?" he asked, his well-waxed eyebrows drawing together in concern.

I nodded, shoving the now-familiar lump in my throat down. "I am. Thanks, Tate." Maybe not quite the truth yet, but close.

"Listen, a guest called down here earlier about a theft in his room?" I said.

Tate nodded, his jowls wobbling up and down. "Carvell. Room 1012."

"Right. Can we comp his room? And maybe give him some credit at the poker tables?"

Tate smiled, showing two dimples in his chubby cheeks. "Darlin', you have your father's instincts when it comes to guest relations," he told me, fingers moving over a hidden keyboard behind the counter.

"Well, keeping gamblers happy isn't all that different from keeping artists happy," I confided.

"Okay, his suite is on the house, and he's got $500 in credits."

"Perfect." While it didn't replace the cash he'd lost, it was at least a start. "Hey, can I ask you something?" I asked, glancing at his computer screen.

"Shoot, dollface." Tate leaned one chubby elbow on the countertop.

"Well, I was wondering if anyone else has reported thefts from their rooms recently?"

"Honey," Tate said, his face breaking into a crooked grin. "We get a few of these a week. People drink, forget where they put stuff, then call down all panicked that they've been 'robbed,'" he said, doing air quotes with his fingers. "Ninety percent of the time, they find whatever they lost shoved down some sofa cushion or tucked under a towel on their bathroom floor."

"What about the other ten percent of the time?" I asked.

Tate shrugged. "Security always handles it. You'd have to ask them."

"Hmm." I had a feeling Alfie wouldn't be quite as forthcoming as Tate. "Could you tell me who you have staying in room 1424?"

"Sure," Tate said, fingers hopping onto the keyboard again. He keyed in the room number, then squinted at the screen. "Actually, it's vacant. We had a couple there last night, but they checked out this morning."

"What time?"

Tate did some more squinting, and I got the distinct impression he was vainly fighting a battle against the need for reading glasses. "Eight-fifteen. Alvin and Shirley Haverstein."

I pursed my lips. Carvell hadn't left his room until nine. While it was still possible that the Haversteins were in on "Mr. Price"'s scheme, I thought it more likely that our mystery high-stakes player had simply given Carvell a random room number. If he'd set up the fake game just as a way to ensure a large amount of cash would be in Carvell's room, the thief knew there was no way the game would ever actually take place.

"Why the interest in this room?" Tate asked.

I shook my head. "Just following up on something for Mr. Carvell. Hey, you don't know anything about high-stakes games being played at the casino, do you?"

Tate frowned. "Like in the VIP rooms?"

"No. I was thinking more private games."

"Oh no. Mr. King would go bananas if he found out about that." Tate paused, his eyes going big and round at his faux pas. "Sorry. I guess it's hard to believe he's really gone."

Damn. There was that lump again. "It's okay," I reassured him, hearing my own voice come out a little higher than I'd intended. "It's something we all have to get used to."

Tate put a hand on my arm and shot me the sympathetic look again. "I'm here, dollface. Any time you wanna talk. Or just grab a cocktail."

I shot him a grateful smile. "Thank you," I said, meaning it. "And I may take you up on that cocktail."

"I'm off at six, girl," Tate shouted as I made my way back to the elevators.

\* \* \*

An hour later I was encased in a big, fluffy white robe and a soothing cucumber mask as I awaited my masseuse, Verlana, in a private room at the Princess Day Spa. I took deep breaths, inhaling the light lavender aromatherapy oil, and willed my mind to empty of all the turbulent emotions I'd experienced over the course of the last few days. I was employing my mother's favorite yoga breathing technique, and just starting to feel my limbs relax, when I heard my name from the spa's lobby.

"I'm sorry, but Ms. King is in a treatment room at the moment," I heard the receptionist say.

"Which one?" a male voice demanded.

My ear perked up, but I didn't recognize the voice.

"Maybe you don't understand," the receptionist replied. "She's scheduled for a massage right now."

"Must be nice," the guy shot back. "But I'm afraid that will have to wait."

"Sir, you can't go back there," I heard the receptionist call.

But whoever it was chose to ignore her as a pair of footsteps took off down the hall, approaching my room.

I tensed, popping up from the treatment table and pulling the cucumber slices off my eyelids just in time to see a man in a grey suit burst through the door.

I let out a yip, sounding like a surprised terrier, and tugged my robe tightly around my middle.

"What is this?" I demanded.

The guy didn't answer, instead asking, "Tessie King?"

I swallowed hard. He was average height, but the tone of his voice and the confident set of his shoulders were commanding enough to fill the room. He had sandy hair, cropped short and dark eyes that were staring at me with an unnerving intensity.

"Who wants to know?" I asked, my eyes cutting from him to the door, wondering just how much of an escape I could stage in the tiny room.

But what he said next killed any thoughts of getting past him.

"Devin Ryder. FBI."

I bit my lip, pulling my robe tighter, suddenly very aware of the fact that I was naked beneath it.

The receptionist chose that moment to finally catch up to my intruder, but at the admission of his affiliation, she didn't linger. Clearly this guy's creds trumped mine.

"So what do you want?" I asked.

"I need to ask you some questions about your father. Richard King."

"Why?" I challenged, hoping my voice came out more confident than I felt. My head was swimming, going over a dozen different scenarios where the FBI might be interested in my father. None of them good.

"When was the last time you saw him?"

"Two years ago."

This caused him pause, one eyebrow rising ever so slightly.

"We weren't overly close," I explained. Then felt silly for feeling like I owed him an explanation. "Why do you want to know?

But again, Agent Ryder didn't answer my question, instead shooting me another of his. "Have you talked to him recently?"

I chewed my lower lip again, trying to remember when the last time I had talked to him was. Christmas? My birthday maybe? "I... I'm not sure."

"You're not sure if you've talked to him or you're not sure it was recently?"

"Right. The second one."

The other eyebrow went up. "You don't seem very confident in that statement."

"Well, you're making me a little nervous," I confided.

The corner of his mouth twitched upward, the small movement transforming his face. I had a feeling that if he actually allowed that smile to grow, it had the potential to be kind of charming.

"Tell me where you were last Tuesday," he said.

I tensed. Tuesday. The day my father died. "I-I don't know. At work. At home. Why?"

"Can anyone verify your whereabouts?"

"Whereabouts?" I shook my head. "Look, what is this? My dad died of a heart attack."

But Agent Ryder just stared at me, his eyes dark, assessing, so penetrating I had the wild thought he could see right through my now very thin feeling robe.

"He *did* die of a heart attack, didn't he?" I asked, dread building somewhere in the center of my chest.

He answered very slowly and deliberately, as if choosing his words carefully. "The M.E. has yet to determine a ruling."

I swallowed. Hard. "Wait. Are you saying there's a chance that my dad's heart attack wasn't from natural causes?" I asked, the words coming out forced even to my own ears. "That there's a chance he was *murdered*?"

Agent Ryder paused. "We're investigating all angles at the moment."

"Oh my God…" the words tumbled out as I tried to wrap my brain around the idea of someone wanting my father dead. While I'd often heard him joke about the competition or the teamsters wanting to "bump him off," the reality that someone actually *had* was jarring enough to make my head spin. "So someone deliberately stopped my dad's heart?"

As was beginning to become an annoying habit, he answered with another question again. "Do you have any idea if your father had a recent disagreement with anyone?" he pressed. "If there was anyone who might have been upset with your father?"

While his face was as void of emotion as any I'd seen at the poker tables, I could feel his eyes taking in every nuance of my posture as I answered. I shifted self-consciously from one bare foot to the other.

"Not especially. But roll the dice. He ran the biggest casino on the South Shore. I'm sure there were a lot of people who resented not having a piece of that pie."

"Like you?"

"*Me*?" I sputtered. "You're kidding, right?"

"You now have the whole pie."

I shut my mouth with a click, eyes narrowing. I took it back. He was *not* charming. "I don't need this pie."

"Really? Because that art school wasn't cheap. You have quite a few student loans."

"Wait—have you been investigating me?" I asked.

His mouth threatened a grin again. "That's kind of my job."

I shook my head. "Look, I do have student loans. So what? So does most of America. I pay my bills. I have a decent job. Trust me, this casino is one thing I don't need."

If he believed me, he made no sign of it, instead switching gears abruptly. "What about your step-mother?"

It took me a moment to realize who he was talking about, the words "mother" and Britton never quite going together in my mind. "You mean Britton?"

He nodded. "Death is a lot less messy than divorce. Especially when there's a pre-nup involved."

I shook my head. "No way. You've got her all wrong," I told him. "There is no way Britton would hurt my father." Defending Britton was the last thing I expected to do. But despite the fact that she dressed somewhere between a stripper and an oversize tween, I couldn't imagine Britton actually hurting my father. As strange as it seemed, I got the impression that she had actually cared about him.

But Agent Ryder didn't seem convinced. "How well do you know Britton?"

I could feel him watching my body language. I did my best not to give anything away. Which was ridiculous because I had nothing incriminating *to* give away.

"We aren't best friends, if that's what you're asking."

"Did you know her before she married your father? I understand she was a cocktail waitress here."

Honestly? This was the first I'd heard of that. I guess I'd never really asked much about their relationship or how they'd met. I shook my head. "No. I never met her before they married."

"But you didn't approve of the marriage?"

I hesitated to answer. The truth was I hadn't. But somehow I felt like that was the wrong answer here.

"My father didn't need my approval," I finally settled on.

"Is that what caused the rift between you?"

"There was no rift," I shot back.

"Yet you haven't seen him in two years."

"I-I've been busy."

"Hmm." Agent Ryder narrowed his eyes at me.

I pulled my robe tighter, willing myself not to fidget under his assessing glare.

Out of the corner of my eyes I saw Verlana hovering in the hallway and jumped on the welcomed interruption.

"Are we done here?" I asked Agent Ryder.

He paused and turned to see Verlana. Then he nodded in my direction. "For now. But I'd appreciate it if you'd stay in town."

Unfortunately, I planned to.

I watched him turn and leave, his back stiff, his posture on alert as if expecting a killer to jump out at him from behind the rack of colored nail polish by the pedicure room.

Verlana entered, apologizing about the delay. I assured her I was fine. But the truth was, there was no way I was going to relax now.

Someone had killed my father.

And it was as clear as the crystal blue waters of the lake at our doorstep that the FBI thought that someone was me.

# CHAPTER FOUR

———

I found myself beating on the penthouse door, sans massage and even more stressed out than before. Britton opened it, and I immediately noticed several men standing behind her, chatting amongst themselves and pointing at the furniture. I must have looked confused at their presence, as Britton waved a hand toward them. "They're the packing crew. What's up, Tessie?"

I cleared my throat, coming into the room. "Before my dad died..." I paused, as much to fight that damned lump again as to find the right words to delicately ask if someone might have wanted him six feet under.

Britton placed a comforting hand on my arm. "I know. It's totally hard, right?"

I nodded, cleared my throat, and tried again. "Did he seem agitated to you? Or maybe upset about anything?"

Britton shrugged. "No more than usual. You know your dad. He was always stressing about some sort of business."

"How *was* business?" I asked.

Again with the shrug. "Same as always. Why?"

"Was he having problems with anyone? Anyone particularly unhappy with him?" I prodded.

Britton's carefully threaded eyebrows twitched as they fought through the Botox to furrow in confusion. "Not that I know of. Everyone loved Dickie. He was just a people kind of person, ya know?" She gazed thoughtfully out the windows at the snow-capped mountains for a moment. "Way too young for a heart attack." Tears formed in her eyes, but she quickly fanned her face with manicured hands and blinked them back.

I waited for her to compose herself before I pressed on. "He was young for a heart attack. That's kind of why I'm wondering if anyone had it out for him. Think. Has anyone picked a fight with him or left any harsh messages?"

She still stared blankly at me.

"Possibly even...I don't know...death threats?" I asked.

I could almost see the light come on as her eyes widened. "Wait. Do you think Dick was murdered?"

As much as I hated to appeal to Britton's sense of drama, I felt myself nodding as I told her about my visit from Agent Ryder.

"Dude," Britton said when I'd finished. She sank back into the deep red, crushed velvet pillows of her sofa, her false eyelashes bobbing up and down at an alarming rate as she digested the idea of her husband being murdered. Finally, her head cocked to the side. "Wait, I don't get it."

I had a feeling Britton uttered that phrase a lot. "Don't get what?" I asked

"Why the FBI? Like, isn't that something our local homicide guys would look into?"

"That's actually a great question." I probably could have held back some of the surprise in that statement, but it didn't seem to faze Britton.

While I was still trying to come up with a logical answer to that, Britton sprang to her feet and grabbed me with both hands.

"I'm so glad you're here to help me with this, Tessie," she said.

I felt my radar perk up. "Help you with what?"

"Well, finding out who killed Dickie, of course," she said, blinking at me like *I* was the dumb one.

"Oh, no. Look, that's way out of my league."

"But, Tessieeeeeee," she said, drawing out the last part of my name like a teenager whining about not being able to take the station wagon out to the mall. "Dick would want us to find the truth. To investigate his death. To avenge his killing!"

"Okay, first off, you've been watching way too much CBS," I told her. "And secondly, I'm not *investigating* anything. That's why the Feds are on the case. I think we should leave this to the experts."

Britton jabbed balled fists to her tiny hips, her face void of expression. "Then why did you come up here?"

Another great question. Damn, she was asking a lot of those lately. "To, uh, I don't know...ask a few questions?" I said, though it came out more as a question itself than an answer. "But that's totally different than investigating."

"Fine," she said, shrugging her slim shoulders. "Then I'll help you ask questions."

I was poised to tell her not just 'no,' but 'oh, hell no,' when my phone vibrated in my purse. Not recognizing the number, I paused to take a cleansing breath before answering.

"Hello?" I snapped. Okay, so it was supposed to be cleansing.

"Girlfriend, Code Sparkle." Tate's familiar voice was full of hushed excitement.

"Code what?"

He released an exasperated sigh into the phone. "Diamonds, duh. I just got wind through the staff grapevine that Mrs. Ditmeyer has her freak-out flag at full mast about the safety of her bling and called security."

I rubbed my temple with my free hand. "And you called me to gossip? I've really got to go."

"Gossip? You know I don't repeat that stuff." He paused, a grin in his voice. "So listen closely the first time."

I couldn't help the unexpected smile that hit my lips. How many times had we shared that exact same joke, pool-side, during summer breaks?

"Anyway," he continued without missing a beat, "Ditmeyer's got her panties in a bunch, and, trust me, she is *not* a client we want to lose. Her husband is the Toilet Tissue Tycoon of the entire West Coast, and they are loaded."

"Toilet Tissue Tycoon?" That smile grew.

"Mr. Softy," he responded.

The commercial's jingle immediately danced through my head, undoubtedly ready to play on repeat throughout my day. "The guy who does the TP tap dance?"

"The one and only. Anyway, his not-so-blushing bride is in room 1470. Gotta run. Kisses!"

I shut my phone off, and Britton immediately started grilling me. "Who was that? What did they want? Can I do anything to help?"

I put up a hand between us, and she clamped her jaw shut. "I just have to un-ruffle some more feathers."

"Give me a few minutes, and I'll help." Britton darted around between the living and dining rooms, flipping magazines, moving knickknacks, and shuffling mail. "Have you seen my phone? Call me so I can find it. Or, just let me use yours." She practically lunged at me.

I clutched my phone to my chest. "Why?"

"I need to call someone to watch the packing guys, so I can go with you."

"Um, no." I saved the 'hell no' for future investigation conversations.

"Why?" she whined. "I should be there if it's another robbery."

"I'm pretty sure it's just feathers this time." I darted out the door to avoid wasting more precious time.

"Call me!" Britton shouted as the door closed.

Yeah. Or not.

\* \* \*

I did a ten count and some yoga breathing in the elevator to regain composure. Not that it did much good. With the day I was having, it would take an entire team of yogis to calm me. Possibly toting martinis. I shoved down thoughts of murder, the FBI, and Britton's "investigations", as the doors opened on yet another posh floor for high rollers.

I straightened my posture as I knocked on the Ditmeyers' door, hoping it would help instill some confidence that I just wasn't quite feeling yet.

"Who is it?" a deep woman's voice barked.

"Security, ma'am." Had my voice not cracked at the end, I might have pulled it off.

The door whipped open as far as the safety bar would allow, and a pair of cloudy grey eyes scanned me up and down several times. With wrinkled lips puckered into a tight grimace, she snorted, "I was told Alfonso Malone, head of security, would attend my needs. Obviously, you are not Mr. Malone."

You think? I smiled past the sarcasm. "I'm Tessie King." I paused, almost choking out the next words. "Owner of the casino."

"Oh." She did nothing to hide the surprise in her voice as she re-scanned me, doing an up and down look again, going from the one white blouse I'd thought to pack to my grey pencil skirt in last year's style. Then her eyes rested on my heels. "One would think that a casino owner would be wearing *real* Manolos. One moment, please."

After slamming the door in my face, I heard her on the phone verifying who I was. This gave me a moment to recover from the shoe diss. I mean, insult my hair, complexion, even my choice of clothes, I'll eventually get past it. But shoes? That was a hard line, and she waddled right over it.

Finally, the security bar rattled, and the portly woman, dressed in what was surely the latest in Egyptian patterned muumuu fashion, allowed me into her suite. Almost as nice as the penthouse, and set up as a slightly smaller version, the balcony doors afforded them yet another amazing view of the mountains. It just never got old.

Mrs. Ditmeyer cleared her throat, dragging me back to the matter at hand.

Her wrinkled, yet perfectly made up face, was creased in a scowl, her eyes mere slits. "I've heard rumors of recent thefts. Rumblings that perhaps our room safe just isn't quite safe enough."

I instantly switched into curator mode. I'd had this type of conversation with many of my artists. Lady, prepare to have your feathers smoothed. "I assure you, every step is being taken to safeguard your personal items while you stay here. We have around the clock security and a fail-proof safe in the lobby, if you still don't feel your belongings are secure." I even forced my sweetest, toothiest smile to my face, as I reluctantly reached out to touch her meaty shoulder in a personal gesture.

She shrugged away from my hand and sauntered over to the wall safe. She paused with her hand on the keypad and shot me a glare over her shoulder.

Taking the hint, I spun around, staring at the door frame as I waited, contemplating different ways to abuse her with my cute Manaylay Blahtniks. (Which were every bit as gorgeous as the real thing, thank you very much.) Finally, she cleared her throat again, and I turned back toward her. In her chubby hands, she held a large blue velvet box.

"I'd like for you to put this in your hotel safe. The fail-proof one," she added. She handed me the box, but kept her firm grip in place. "This has been handed down in my husband's family for many generations. We're having portraits taken at the lake this weekend, and I plan to wear it for the sitting." She opened the lid, and my eyes were assaulted by the sparkling facets of huge teardrop diamonds on a large gold rope necklace. While it wasn't exactly my style, I could only imagine the price tag of such an elaborate piece. My fingers twitched at the thought of touching the stones.

As though reading my mind, Mrs. Ditmeyer stated, "Please note on the paperwork with the office downstairs that the last insurance estimate was just over $2.5 million."

Trying to camouflage my gasp caused me to inhale my own saliva. In a feeble attempt to cover my choking fit, I forced a couple of real coughs. "Darn this Spring cold," I covered, unconvincingly.

Ditmeyer let out a cynical snort as she escorted me back into the hallway. "Please have the front desk call me when it is safely locked away." The curtness of her statement was punctuated with the door slamming in my face.

Oh, the glamorous life of a casino owner.

# CHAPTER FIVE

———

Acting cool under pressure was never really a strong suit at any point in my life. So, carrying two-and-a-half million dollars' worth of diamonds across a casino floor to the front desk was making me break out in a sweat. Sure, I'd dealt in fairly expensive pieces of art at the gallery. But they were affixed to a wall, surrounded by security cameras, and viewed mainly by collectors and artists. I felt like every crook on the entire South Shore could smell what I held in my hands, knew how much it was worth, and was stalking me at that very moment. Needless to say, when Tate snuck up on me, I screamed like a little girl. Thankfully, the clanging of slot machines and squeals of winners masked it well.

Once my surroundings came back into focus, and I was able to draw breath again, I dug my nails into his arm. "What the hell, man?"

One perfectly plucked brow rose. "You are jumpier than a straight man in a truck stop bathroom."

I slowly moved my gaze down to the large velvet box clutched to my chest then raised it back to meet his meaningfully.

His jaw dropped. "Is that Old Lady Ditmeyer's?"

I bobbed my head slightly, as I suspiciously glanced around at everyone within earshot. "It's her necklace. She wanted it put in the safe. But I feel like I need an armed guard carrying this thing around."

An evil grin curled the corners of his lips and danced in his eyes. "If you give me a peek, I'm your man."

"Nice try," I told him. Just help me get this thing to the front desk and out of my hands."

He shrugged. "Fine. My break is over anyhow, so I'm headed that way."

Keeping a death grip on the box with one hand, I threaded the other through the crook of Tate's arm, allowing him to lead me through the crowd. I knew if anyone threatened us, he would more than likely scream and toss me in front of him, but I felt better at least having company.

I released a huge sigh of relief as he buzzed me behind the desk and unlocked the outer door to the vault.

"You're on your own now, dollface." He blew air kisses as the heavy door closed between us.

A very tall, heavily armed man stood in the doorway. He did the same up and down thing Mrs. Ditmeyer had graced me with.

*Go on, diss my shoes, too. I just carried a diamond necklace across a crowded casino. I am Wonder Woman.*

He put a hand to his ear, then his stone face immediately morphed into a bright smile. "The front desk just messaged me on my com. It's a pleasure to meet you, Ms. King."

Amazing how meeting the boss could turn any face into a butt-kissing smile.

"Likewise," I lied. "I've, uh, got something for the safe," I said, gesturing to the box.

He turned and punched in a code which opened the gate, then used his key and a combination to unlock the glass door beyond that. "Looks like you'll need one of the bigger safe-deposit boxes for that. Here is the paperwork." He dropped a large binder full of papers on a sleek metal desk. "And I'll send the code up to Mrs. Ditmeyer with a messenger. She will need that code, and either me or another guard with a key, to get her package."

I filled out the 15 pages of documentation to the best of my ability and watched as Rent-A-Cop locked the necklace safely away. I felt myself relax and released a huge breath I didn't even know I'd been holding. Suddenly, I felt like me again.

Scanning the front desk for Tate as I left, I was a teeny bit glad he had wandered off again. After the day I'd had, room service and a long nap were in order. I was just heading up to my room to indulge in both when I spotted Rafe signing autographs in the vestibule.

For a moment I weighed my options. Sleep or hot snowboarder? When he saw me walking through the lobby, he smiled and waved me over.

*Hot snowboarder it is.*

I told myself that snowboarder crushes were so last decade. While his gorgeous green eyes might make the butterfly population in my gut number in the flock range, my taste in men ran more toward those with a real job and no groupies. I glanced around at all of the barely legal girls clustered around him, undoubtedly sporting a combined IQ of less than one hundred. Which helped Adult-me fight for domination over crushing-Teen-me at the last second. "Hey, you," I yelled across the crowd.

"Tessie," he called out, "I'm just finishing up. Give me a sec." One of the bleach blondes flashed me the stink eye as she pulled her shirt open, nearly exposing more than I cared to see in her haste. Rafe proceeded to sign his name across her cleavage.

Classy.

After kissing the love-starved girl on the forehead, he swatted her butt as he left the swarm. "You girls have a wonderful evening, and I'll see you on the mountain tomorrow. Okay?"

They all nodded emphatically, like life-sized Barbie bobble heads in designer ski gear.

Rafe scooped me into a quick hug, and I could swear they all sent dirty looks my way. Teen-me loved it.

"How you doing?" he asked, his eyes full of concern.

"Good," I nodded, doing my best to look convincing.

"Wow, you're a terrible actress."

Apparently my best wasn't that good. I grinned at him. "Okay, I'm having what could be in the running for top three worst days of my life. Right behind getting spinach dip stuck in my braces for my eighth grade prom pictures and crashing my Honda Civic into the back of a loaded fertilizer truck when I was sixteen."

Rafe pulled me in for another hug, though I swear I heard him stifle a laugh. "I'm sorry, Tess. It's gonna get better."

"Thanks," I said, reluctantly leaving the warmth of his aftershave scented embrace. "Hey, can I ask you something?"

"Shoot," Rafe told me, crossing his arms over his chest in a way that highlighted his pro-athlete biceps. I momentarily lost my train of thought, staring at them.

"Uh, right, um...you said at the cemetery that my dad's heart attack seemed unlikely. That he didn't seem to have a weak heart."

Rafe's eyes clouded, his lashes making long shadows on his cheeks as his gaze hit the ground. "I guess none of us know when something like that is going to sneak up on us."

"Right. I'm wondering if maybe it wasn't bad health that snuck up on him."

He frowned. "What do you mean?"

"Did my dad seem different to you?" I asked. "Agitated or distracted by anything?"

Rafe's frown deepened, his arms folding tighter as he shifted his stance. "Not that I noticed. Your dad was business as usual right up until..." His voice dropped off, brow pinched together with concern. "Why do you ask?"

I was so caught up in his intense green eyes, I almost blurted out that I thought my dad had been murdered. Fortunately, I caught myself in time.

"Just curious about my father's last few days." I nearly choked on the finality in those words. Regret started budding in my gut, pulling my strong façade apart. Tears threatened to spill, but I quickly swiped them away.

Rafe reached out a hand, running his thumb gently under my chin. His touch and look of sincere concern melted Teen-me into a puddle of heart-doodling goo. When he glanced at me through his long, dark lashes, flashing me a smile that popped dimples in both cheeks, the warmth flared to meltdown status.

"I'm glad you decided to stick around," he told me.

I felt myself blushing under his gaze and told myself he was just being polite.

"Yeah, well, it turns out there are a few items of unfinished business that my dad left behind," I hedged, not sure how far the rumor mill extended.

"I heard," Rafe said, answering that question for me. "*Boss*," he added with a wink.

I shook my head as Teen-me and Adult-me battled over the new round of butterflies getting giddy in my stomach over that wink. "Just on paper. And it's only temporary."

"Well, I guess I better take advantage of your company while I have it then," he said, grinning his charm-the-pants-off-the-groupies smile. "Hit the powder with me tomorrow? If memory serves me, you were hell on a board."

Before I could stop myself, I heard my crushing Teen-self saying, "Sure. Sounds like fun." I even punctuated it with a girly giggle of unknown origin.

His face lit up like Christmas. I made a mental note to have a stern talk with my teenage self about rekindling old crushes. At a complete loss for what to say next, I was saved by the bell, or chirping cell phone as it was. I pulled it from my purse, checking the readout. Britton. Good God, what now?

"Sorry, I have to take this." I waggled my finger at the boob-signing pen he still clutched, and he handed it to me. After scrawling my phone number in his palm, with what I hoped to be permanent ink, and waving good-bye, I answered my phone while I headed to the elevators.

"Hi, Britton."

"Oh Em Gee, Tessie," she wailed. "I need to talk to you, like now. I know what killed my Dickie!"

I blinked at the phone. "What?"

"Just come upstairs," she said, hiccupping out a sob. "I'll explain everything." Then she hung up.

While I was beginning to think everything in Britton's world was overly-dramatized, I'll admit that I practically ran the last few steps to the elevator. By the time I got to the penthouse door, all kinds of scenarios were racing through my head.

Britton let me in, black mascara-filled tears streaked down her face. I could see the packing crew still hard at work down the hall, moving boxes from room to room. But Britton ignored them, grabbing me in a tight hug as she sobbed into my shoulder.

"I was going through some of Dick's things as they were boxing it all up," she sob-hiccupped again. "I thought maybe there'd be some clue in there somewhere as to who killed him."

"Was there?" I couldn't help my curiosity asking.

She shook her head. "Not who. But I did find what."

"What was it?"

"Well, the EMT's took all of his medications and stuff…" She paused as she inhaled a staccato breath along with a nose full of snot. She continued in full bawling mode. "...when they took his body."

I found myself patting her back and desperately searching the penthouse for a box of tissues for the next nasal event.

Her red-rimmed eyes brightened a bit. "But they left his DynoDrink mix."

"His Dyno-what?" I handed her a dish towel, hoping she'd use it instead of power-snorting.

She dabbed her eyes daintily, clearly not realizing her mascara was way beyond dabbing. "DynoDrink," she continued. "It's this super-food health powder you mix with water. Dick drank two every day. Anyway, I'm sure that's how he was poisoned."

"My dad drank health shakes?" I had a hard time picturing the old school, martini and a cigar guy I remembered downing wheatgrass.

But Britton nodded. "Rafe got him into it. He does endorsements for the stuff."

Which was almost as surprising. I hadn't realized he and my dad were close, let alone on the level to share health tips.

"Okay, I'll bite. What makes you so sure this stuff was what killed him?"

"He collapsed twenty minutes after drinking it. That's exactly the time it takes the average man's digestive tract to fully break down the proteins and disperse them to the red blood cells."

I blinked at her.

"I googled."

Of course she did. "I'm not sure that's exactly conclusive evidence," I said, playing devil's advocate.

"Oh, and it smells funny. Like caviar gone bad, you know?" Britton said, scrunching up her nose.

No, I didn't, my diet running more toward canned tuna than caviar. But, I took a whiff from the plastic canister she held out to me. It looked almost full, like a freshly opened canister. But a distinct odor of dead fish and something I couldn't quite put a finger on came wafting back up at me. I took the container from her and read the ingredients, not entirely sure it hadn't started out smelling that way.

"Okay," I said as I handed the canister back to her. "Let's say, for argument's sake, this killed him. Who knew he drank the stuff?"

"Gosh, everyone. Dickie was so into it, he tried to get anyone who'd listen to drink the stuff. Said it gave him total energy. Better than Viagra even."

I didn't know which one disturbed me more, the thought of my father being gone or the image of him having sex. "TMI territory again, Britton."

She gave me a sheepish look. "Sorry."

I grabbed the drink mix, turning the canister over in my hands. By now it had been handled by Britton, me, the moving guys, and who knew how many household staff. *If* it had been the murder weapon and *if* the killer had left any fingerprints, they were long gone now. Which just left us once again with more questions than answers.

Not the least of which was what had Richard King done that had someone angry enough to kill him?

# CHAPTER SIX

———

I left Britton with her packing crew and health shake theories, promising to call her later. As I rode the elevator, my rumbling stomach reminded me I hadn't eaten since breakfast. I stopped at the sixth floor, detouring to the right where a small restaurant occupied the back of the casino. The Minstrel Lounge was already filling up, a Frank Sinatra impersonator on the small stage crooning to all who entered. Dead center was a bar set up to match the ambiance. Leather stools surrounded a stainless counter with neon signs touting drink specials and vodka brands. The staff was all dressed up like hip Rat Pack clones in dark suits, funky hats and skinny ties. I instantly knew this was my dad's vision. That pang of regret niggled at me again, telling me I really should have visited more often.

The maître de approached me. "How many in your party this evening?" As I raised one finger, a look of disdain crossed his elongated, goateed face. We wove through the tables with him mumbling under his breath about the buffet downstairs.

I followed him to a tiny, dimly-lit corner table, the men's restroom on one side and the hustle and bustle of the kitchen doors on the other.

*Fabulous.*

I would've asked to move to the bar if he hadn't tossed my menu on the table and darted away. Accepting my less than prime location, I sat down and looked over my choices. The menu was the same nod to the sixties as the ambience, meat and potatoes dominating the meal choices. Which sounded like heaven at the moment. I was vacillating between the All-American cheeseburger and the Hometown meatloaf with garlic mashed potatoes when the Sinatra impersonator paused between songs.

"This one goes out to Richard King," Old Blue Eyes said.

I immediately got that familiar lump in my throat.

"Like him, it's an oldie but goodie. Here's to you, Mr. King, wherever you are," he said. Then he started crooning "Thanks for the Memory."

I found myself silently singing along, my mind tripping over my own old memories of my dad as my gaze wandered over the patrons of the restaurant. It wasn't packed, but there was a decent dinner crowd gathering. The bar was still sparsely populated. I watched as a young Joe Pesci look-alike sat down on one of the leather stools. Short, dark hair, dressed all in black, even sporting a leather dress coat. I found myself grinning as the guy greeted the bartender with the same, "Hey, how ya doin'? Right, right?" as Pesci's character in *My Cousin Vinny*.

"Pesci" ordered a drink, sipped at it, listened to the Sinatra impersonator a bit. He'd almost faded from my thoughts when I spotted Buddy Weston walk in and sit on the stool next to him.

I narrowed my eyes. What was Weston doing here? Britton had made it pretty clear that he wasn't welcome.

As he slipped off his suit coat, the glare from his signature silk shirt nearly lit up the area around him. I was about to get up and tell Weston to take a hike when another man sat down on the other side of Mr. Pesci. As he stole a wary glance over his shoulder, I recognized the freckled face of the casino's valet. He leaned in, addressing both Pesci and Weston.

I raised an eyebrow. Now this was interesting. I desperately wanted to hear what they were whispering but couldn't figure a feasible way to get closer without being recognized. Or looking like I was shamelessly eavesdropping. I watched as Weston pulled an envelope from the jacket draped over his arm and passed it under the counter to Pesci. The valet yanked it between them. I saw both men flipping through the contents but wasn't close enough to confirm what it was. Whatever it was, they both seemed satisfied, as Pesci nodded at Weston, clapping him jovially on the back. Weston slipped off his stool, threw his jacket on, and walked away. Downing their drinks, Pesci and the freckled valet followed him out the door a few minutes later.

Whatever that exchange had been about, it didn't feel right. I had no idea who Pesci was, but I couldn't imagine a good reason for the owner of a competing casino to be passing an envelope to one of our employees. I made a mental note to pull the freckle-faced guy's employee file later.

I was mulling over the different possibilities for the envelope's contents when Tate cleared his throat in front of me.

"Tessie King, as I live and breathe, there are better ways to pick up guys." He bobbed his head toward the men's room door.

I pulled myself out of my thoughts and shook my head. "Apparently, if you dine alone in this establishment, you are just begging for the worst table in the house." I glanced around at the empty prime spots, heaving a sigh.

Tate grabbed my hand, yanking me to my feet. He pulled me behind him to a table with a spectacular view of the lake and the sun setting on the horizon. Then he turned and loudly proclaimed directly at the maître de, "No one puts Tessie King in a corner."

I watched with a little more than my fair share of contentment as the man's goateed jaw dropped to his chest. He nearly fell over several other customers as he darted to our table.

"Whatever you want, Ms. King, it's on the house," he babbled as he smoothed the table cloth and swatted non-existent crumbs to the floor.

Tate's eyes lit up. "She'll have an apple-tini, please." He leaned across the table and whispered, "Did you want one, too?"

I nodded, "Sure, why not."

"Okay, so two, please. And don't be a stranger."

"And a burger for me," I added as the maître de walked away.

He bowed slightly toward the table in acknowledgement, before turning to jog to the bar. Leaning in, he whispered in the bartender's ear. The man mixed our drinks with such fervor you'd have thought James Bond himself had ordered them. Shaken, not stirred. Within seconds, they were gently placed on our table.

Tate lifted the drink to his lips, inhaling the aroma, a smile reaching his eyes as he took the first sip. His lashes fluttered as he set the glass reluctantly back in front of him. "The best drink ever made."

I couldn't help but grin. Tate was a full-of-life breath of fresh air that I sorely needed today.

"Speaking of drinks...Tate, did you know that my dad was drinking health shakes?"

"Ugh. I'm drinking the nectar of the gods, and you bring up DynoDrink?" He shuddered, clasping both hands around the fragile stem of his glass. "Mr. King tried to get me to try it once. No dice. I'll die young enjoying these, thank you very much." He savored another sip of the bright green concoction.

"What about Rafe?" I pried, not really sure what made me bring him up.

"What about him?" Tate appeared puzzled for a second until the bartender slid a second round in front of us. I hadn't even touched mine, so I chalked it up to extreme butt kissing.

"Britton said Rafe got my dad into them?"

Tate nodded. "Rafe is a spokesperson for DynoDrink. He'd give your dad a fresh can every few days from his stash."

I wondered if the fresh canister my dad had taken his dose from on the day he died had come from Rafe. A niggle of unease at that thought played at the back of my mind. "Was Rafe around on the weekend my dad died?"

Tate frowned, cocking his head to the side in thought. "He was. Big snowboarding competition on the mountain that weekend. His publicist was in town, too. I'm pretty sure he was either tied up with the tournament, or tied up by her." He paused to take a sip. "Metaphorically *and* literally, if I were to guess. For a girl, she's kinda hot." He pointed to a huge poster at the end of the bar I couldn't believe I hadn't even noticed.

Cardboard Rafe was nearly life-sized with a myriad of smaller pictures surrounding him. In most, a tiny blonde woman was draped on his arm, gorgeous, perfect teeth, not a hair out of place. She inspired instant hatred in me—by both Teen and Adult-me.

"Why do you ask, sugar?" Tate asked.

I shook my head. "It's nothing. I'm just...thinking about my dad, that's all," I said, not quite ready to share Britton's deadly shake theory yet.

Tate clucked his tongue and did a head-tilted, lips-pursed, pity-face.

Smiling, I assured him, "I'm okay. Promise."

He stuck a little finger in my face, and I was forced by a long ago pact to lock mine with his. "Pinky swear," I added.

"Your dad was an amazing man. I know you guys didn't really see eye to eye on, well, most things, but he loved you. I know that for sure."

I let him take a few sips of his drink while pondering his words. "Really? How are you so sure?"

"How many summers did we spend together? Ten, maybe? My mom absolutely adored working for your dad. The entire week before you came out for your summer visit, he practically had the staff on lockdown, cleaning and prepping twenty-four-seven. Everything had to be in tip-top shape before you got here. The pool was always his main focus since he knew how much time you spent there."

Pleasant memories filtered past my stubborn pride. I allowed myself to feel the excitement of the summer when I was twelve. I had walked through the pool gate and seen the huge, twisting slide Dad had installed. When I turned fifteen he'd added a new wave pool. I'd tucked those memories so far back in my subconscious, they'd been lost behind all of the times when he'd forgotten to call on Christmas, or send a card when I'd gotten straight A's, or announced that he was marrying someone just a few years older than me. Seeing tears flowing down Tate's face made me realize he was mirroring my own.

I swiped at my eyes. "Sorry."

He reached for my hands. "Oh, honey, don't be. I was worried that you hadn't let them out already. You should be very proud of all that your dad accomplished. Not to mention how much he appreciated each and every person who worked for him. He made sure he knew each employee, their family, their needs. Why do you think I was always here? Mom couldn't afford a babysitter after Dad bailed. The staff became my second family." Tate forced a smile to his face.

I wavered between loving and loathing my father but jumped at the chance to make Tate smile for real by changing the subject. "How about we toast to the fabulous individuals we are now despite our jacked-up childhoods." We raised our glasses, clinked them together, each enjoying a big sip. Okay, so mine was more like a chug, but I'd earned it.

"Oh, fun fact!" Tate blurted. "Did you know this very table was your dad's favorite? He came up here almost every evening for a cigar, a drink, and to enjoy the fabulous view."

I turned just in time to watch the last deep orange glimmer of daylight fade behind the mountain. Had my burger not showed up at the same moment, it might have prompted some deep connection with my past. As it was, my stomach won out, and I practically dove into the plate.

Tate stared across the table as I devoured my burger, his eyes wide and a slight Elvis tic tugging at his upper lip.

"What?" I asked between bites.

"Oh, just that I've never seen anyone as small as you put food away like that. I mean, I've watched a show on television where piranhas dissected a whole cow. I'm getting the same vibe here, sweetness. I hope you don't eat this way on a date."

I put the remaining few bites back on my plate and swallowed what was left in my mouth. I pondered retaliating with some of his more embarrassing moments that I'd witnessed once we had hit puberty. The slumber parties where I'd woken to see his hair pre-product-enhanced, the breakups I'd helped him through with red snotty noses and lots of tissues, the time he thought a Speedo was a good bathing suit choice and I had to warn him that his junk was on the loose. The options were nearly endless. I opened my mouth to rehash the highlights, but his cheeks were already rosy. He'd obviously just hiked the same memory lane.

"Touché." He raised his glass, tossed me a playful wink, and took a sip. "You always have been more like family to me. You know, I think we need a girl's night before you leave."

"Sure, why not?" I finished my burger slowly, pondering what the week would hold for me as temporary owner of a casino.

"Omigod." Tate's eyes rounded, and a smile lit his face. "There's a male revue show at the Deep Blue tomorrow night. We are so going."

"I don't know…"

"We don't have to close the place down. We'll just go check out the man-meat and make an informed decision on whether it's worth wasting our whole night."

"Well," I tried to piece together a reason to decline, but the truth was, I did need a girl's night with Tate. And the fact that it was at the Deep Blue might give me an excuse to question Weston about his odd appearance here at the bar tonight. "Okay, it's a date." I finished off my drink and stifled a yawn.

"Girl, you must be wiped out after the day you've had."

"Yeah, I think I'm going to have to head up to my room."

Tate stood and extended his arm. "Allow me to escort you to your elevator, m'dame."

"Why, thank you, kind sir." I stood and slid my arm through his. With the medieval theme of the casino, there had been many nights where Tate had played the knight in shining armor for me. If only he'd been straight. Or I'd been a guy.

Tate prattled on about the dancers at the Deep Blue Revue. Apparently he knew a few of them and had high hopes of us going backstage. I liked a half-naked man just as much as Tate did, but I wasn't quite sure I wanted to go behind the scenes. Sometimes when you lift the veil, and the mystery is gone, there's just no going back. He kissed me on the forehead and pushed me into the open elevator.

"Get some rest, girl. You've got darker circles than most raccoons." We air kissed as the doors closed.

The elevator rocketed me to my suite, and I was never so grateful to see my bed turned down and ready for me to slip into it. But as soon as I walked into the room, I felt the hairs on the back of my neck stand at attention. I froze, my eyes quickly scanning the room. Everything looked just as I'd left it. With the exception of the turn-down service and the fresh towels. I fought the urge to call out, "Hello." Clearly I was alone. Clearly I was paranoid. Clearly I'd had too much apple-tini on too little sleep.

I shook my head, fighting down the feeling that something was off as I unzipped my suitcase. I grabbed a T-shirt and pair of little pink shorts with bunnies on them to sleep in. Then I took the hottest, longest shower I possibly could, staying under the water until my fingers pruned and my skin went a rosy pink. I towel dried my hair as I walked to the windows, staring out at the twinkling lights of the miniature Vegas-like strip below and the hulking white mountains beyond. Thoughts of my dad, both good and not so stellar, warred with each, swirled together with health shakes, FBI agents, and the question of who hated my dad enough to end his life. Unfortunately, the twinkling lights held as few answers for me as the rest of the day had, and I finally shut the curtains, bringing darkness and hopefully sleep with them.

As I snuggled under the covers finally ready to succumb to sleep, something at the back of my mind suddenly startled me back awake. It hit me what was off in the room.

I'd left my suitcase unzipped when I'd left with Tate that morning. Someone had gone through my things.

# CHAPTER SEVEN

———

The next morning, Britton called bright and early, inviting me to breakfast at the penthouse. I blame it on the fact that I was pre-coffee that I couldn't think of an excuse not to. So an hour later I found myself staring at a plate of eggs and freshly cut fruit while Britton mixed mimosas.

"I heard you visited Dickie's place last night," she said, handing me a glass.

I paused, forkful of cantaloupe melon halfway to my lips. "His place?"

"The Minstrel's Lounge. Jordan said you sat at Dickie's favorite table."

I set the cantaloupe down, not sure I could get it past the lump in my throat. "Who's Jordan?" I asked, deflecting the emotion.

"The maître de. He said you and Tate were pounding back drinks like there was no tomorrow."

"Goatee Guy told you that?" I asked.

Britton snorted. "'Goatee Guy.' I like that. His facial hair is, like, total last year, right? Yeah, anyway, no, he told Jake who works the late shift at the baccarat tables, who told Amy the cocktail waitress, who told my friend Gigi who was up here doing my nails this morning." She paused, holding up all ten digits, currently painted hot pink with little white flower designs. "Cute, right?"

I nodded. "Fab. Almost as fab as the idea that the entire staff now thinks their boss is a drunk. 'Pounding back' the apple-tinis?" I set my mimosa down, concentrating on my eggs instead.

But Britton waved me off with one hand full of designer nails. "Don't sweat it. Everyone knows you're grieving."

"Hmm." I gave a non-committal grunt, trying to keep my mind focused on eggs lest that lump come back.

"Anyhoo, how did it go yesterday?" she asked.

I shrugged. "The lounge was nice. Very Richard King."

Britton rolled her eyes. "No, silly. I meant the *other* thing."

"What 'other thing'?" I asked, narrowing my eyes at her.

Britton shook her head and did a well-duh face. "The investigation into Dickie's murder."

"You mean the one the FBI is doing?" I said around a bite of eggs.

"Riiiight." She winked at me.

"I'm serious. I'm not investigating."

"Uh-huh."

"No, really."

"Gotcha." More winking.

My turn to roll my eyes. "Whatever happened to my dad, I'm sure the authorities are looking into it," I told her. And I was. I just wasn't sure exactly *who* they were looking at.

"Well, while you *weren't* investigating," she continued, "I was going through Dickie's den for any clues to who might have had it in for him."

As much as I was totally leaving this to the authorities, I couldn't help asking, "What did you find?"

She shook her head, her blonde ponytail swishing behind her. "Nada."

"Fab." I shoveled some more eggs in.

"Don't you see?" she asked, blinking rapidly at me. "There should have been *something* there. I mean, he had zero papers in his desk, zero correspondence, nothing related to the casino."

"What are you saying?" I asked, the hairs on the back of my neck starting to prick again.

"I think someone's been in here. Someone cleaned his desk out of anything incriminating."

I opened my mouth to speak, but Britton was faster.

"And I don't mean the housekeeping crew."

I shut my mouth with a click. That had been exactly what I was thinking. Maybe it was possible that Ellie was overly zealous in cleaning out his den after he passed. Maybe the packing crew had got to the desk before Britton did. Maybe my dad hadn't wanted to bring his business home with him.

Or maybe Britton was right.

"I think someone was in my room last night," I blurted.

Britton gasped and pointed one hot pink fingernail at me. "Shut up. Was anything missing?" she asked.

I shook my head. "Not that I could tell," I said, then relayed the suitcase incident. "Obviously the housekeeping staff had been there, but I know they're under strict policy not to touch personal items. I highly doubt anyone would violate that just to zip up a suitcase."

Britton's eyes never left mine, but she stood and grabbed the glass carafe from the counter. "More mimosa?"

I put a hand over my glass. My head was spinning, and it wasn't even noon. "No thanks." I paused as she got up, taking in her outfit for the first time. "But I have to ask. What's with the legwarmers and tights?"

She beamed and ran a hand over the bright pink spandex leotard. "The 80's are coming back. This was in the shop window last week and Dickie said..." The smile tumbled from her face. "He said they were perfect for me since I'm an old soul and stuff." She cleared her throat and forced a pretend smile. "You should come with me to the Pilates class at the Medieval Torture Chamber this morning."

I choked past the bite of egg I'd just swallowed. "The what now?"

"The gym. Everything down there is state of the art. And the hot tub is divine." She released a soft sigh.

*Now she's talking my language.*

"I might have to check it out," I replied casually, trying not to be too committal to anything other than the hot tub.

"Anyway, you should totally tell Alfie about your room." She sat down across the table from me again and propped her chin on her hands.

"Tell him what? That I think someone zipped my suitcase?" I shook my head. "I'll just pay closer attention. I mean, it's possible I just didn't remember zipping it."

But Britton shook her head. "Uh-uh. No way. It's too much of a coincidence. Someone was in there, Tessie." She paused, pondering that thought. "You know, it had to have been someone with a master key, just like the heist in Carvell's room."

"Heist? Seriously, you need to lay off the TV dramas, Britton."

"He checked out, by the way. Carvell," she continued. "Said Mr. Price and all of the drama unsettled him, and he'd feel more comfortable at the Deep Blue."

"Really?" I dabbed my mouth with the napkin and draped it across my empty plate. The fact that the mysterious Mr. Price had cost us a client didn't sit well with me. And I'm sure it wouldn't have sat well with my dad, either.

And as much as I thought Britton was over dramatizing the incident in my room, the idea that Mr. Price might still be in my casino running around with a master key left me feeling just a tad too vulnerable for my liking. Maybe I would visit Alfie after all.

"Oh, shoot!" Britton said, looking down at her cell. "Pilates is starting in ten. I gotta get going." She paused, turning a bright-eyed stare on me that reminded me of a puppy waiting for someone to throw the ball. "Want to join me?"

"Um, yeah, not today. I, uh, I've got some things to take care of," I mumbled.

Her eyes fell, but she quickly covered it with a bright, forced smile. "Sure. Call me later?"

"I will," I promised, rising and hitting the penthouse door before she could drag me to the Torture Chamber.

I got in the elevator and contemplated the different floor buttons. Security was on the second floor. I mentally played out the conversation I'd have with Alfie about my room break-in. None of the possibilities had me coming out sounding anything other than paranoid. What I needed was something solid. Some real evidence that Mr. Price had been... or still was... at the casino. I thought back to the info Mr. Carvell had given security. He mentioned that he'd met Price at the poker tables. It wouldn't hurt to at least go ask around, see if any of the dealers had seen Mr. Price.

I hit the button for the main floor, riding down to the lobby. The casino floor was fairly busy for midmorning. I weaved my way through the noisy slot machines and found the modestly populated poker tables. I started at one that was empty, asking the dealer wearing a name tag that read Sal if he'd seen Carvell chatting with anyone. Luckily, Carvell was a familiar enough fixture that Sal knew exactly who I was talking about. Unluckily, he didn't remember him speaking with anyone in particular on the night in question. I thanked him, moving on to another dealer near the back of the room. But before I got there, a commotion at one of the busier tables grabbed my attention.

A tall, lanky dealer leaned across one of the high-stakes tables, hands fumbling between two players who were shouting heated words at one another. If I had to guess, they were seconds from exchanging their words for blows.

I darted over, and the dealer's face brightened. "Ms. King, Security is tied up with a large cash delivery. Can you find someone to help?"

"What's the problem, gentlemen?" I shoved myself between the two bulky older men, one in a ball cap and dark glasses, and the other in a nice pin-striped suit. They continued grabbing around me, pushing on each other. I allowed them to jostle me about for a few seconds, trying to remain calm and speak soothingly, until a fist hurtled past my face. Fearing the losing end of a sucker punch, I shoved my fingers in my mouth and whistled loudly, fairly pleased with the resounding trill.

Suit Man backed up a few steps and said, "That son-of-a-bitch stole my chips!"

Ball Cap Guy smoothed his bunched Yankee's T-shirt with a pair of sweaty hands, leaving streaks on it. "I did nothing of the sort," he whined, his voice high and tense.

I honed in on the details of each man, just like my father had taught me, taking them each in from head to toe. To spot a liar, you needed to watch for tells, just like in poker.

Suit Guy looked me straight in the eyes, his gaze cool and calm, while Ball Cap Guy was sweating profusely, shifting his weight from foot to foot, with his arms crossed defiantly over his chest.

"May I see the contents of your pockets?" I politely requested of Suit Man.

"What?" He rolled his eyes and snorted as he shoved his hands into his armpits. "This isn't the frickin' Hokey Pokey, Sweetheart. I just want the five hundred dollars in chips this asshole stole from my stack."

I gave him my sweetest smile. "Sir, we have a lot of surveillance." I waved my hand toward the surplus of hanging black balls. "We have a dedicated camera trained on each of these tables. All it will take is a quick trip up to the security office to straighten this out. Or, we can bypass the formality, and you can show me what you have in your jacket pockets, please."

I watched as Alfie walked up behind Suit Man, pausing when he saw me.

But Suit Man didn't see him, instead focusing on me as he poked a finger to my chest. "I don't gotta show you a damn thing, bitch."

That did it. Alfie was at the man's side in one long stride, yanking the man's shirt collar. "That's no way to talk to a lady. She said 'please,' but if you want to do this the hard way, you can deal with me."

Suit Man slowly turned to meet Alfie's glare, his face turning a shade of pale. "I…I was just playing with her."

"And your pocket contents?" Alfie raised a hairy brow, their noses almost touching.

"I, uh, have extra chips in there for later."

"Let me guess," I scoffed. "Five hundred dollars' worth?"

Alfie slipped his hand in the guy's coat and counted the chips. "What a coincidence, eh?" Amusement glinted in his eyes but didn't quite make it to the rest of his stony expression. "I think we need to have a chat in my office."

As Suit Man was dragged toward the elevators, Ball Cap Guy zealously shook my hand. "Thank you so much, ma'am. That guy was fu…um, crazy."

With my ego fully inflated, I could almost feel my Wonder Woman cape fluttering behind me as I watched Ball Cap Guy return to the poker table.

"Impressive."

I spun around to find Agent Ryder directly behind me. The amusement on his face matched Alfie's—somehow looking like it was at my expense even though *I* was the one who'd unmasked the cheater.

"Um, thanks?" My face flushed warm.

"How'd you guess it was the guy in the suit that was lying?"

I shrugged. "Easy. He was too calm. When someone's telling the truth, they have no reason to hide their emotions. Ball Cap was nervous as heck, which is the normal reaction to being falsely accused. Suit Guy was wearing a poker face."

"Sounds like you've spent a lot of time at these tables yourself," he observed.

I shook my head. "Not in a long time," I mumbled, shoving those old memories down. I quickly changed the subject before thoughts of my dad could come flooding in again. "I didn't know you were still at the casino."

"Just interviewing some of your dad's…well, *your* employees." He arched a brow at me.

*My employees.* I took a deep breath and stated, "Right. Temporarily. I'll be gone in a few days."

Nodding, he muttered, "Of course."

"But, while I'm here and in charge, tell me why the FBI is investigating this instead of the local police," I asked, crossing my arms across my chest and doing my best to project some air of authority.

He stared directly into my eyes for several seconds, never flinching or blinking, before saying, "I'm part of the Nevada Organized Crime Task Force."

"'Organized' crime?" I repeated.

But he ignored the question mark at the end my statement, instead continuing with his carefully worded response. "We've been looking into your father and his business for some time now. Seems he's been doing some creative bookkeeping and has more than one interesting business connection."

"Define 'interesting' and 'creative'?" I asked, narrowing my eyes at his choice of adjectives.

"Mafia."

"That's crazy!" I sputtered on impulse, swiping my hand through the air. "My dad isn't…wasn't like that. A little rough around the edges, maybe, but not…" I trailed off, fully digesting what I was saying. I knew the father who doted on me two weeks out of the summer. I knew the stories my mother told me about a man who paid more attention to his precious casino than his own daughter. I knew the dad who called sporadically, sometimes at one o'clock in the morning just to chat. I knew the hero Tate painted him to be. I'd even been granted a peek into his softer side via Britton. But, what I didn't know was the kind of a businessman he was.

And Agent Ryder must have guessed that as his own eyes narrowed now, studying my face.

"Are you okay?" he asked, something akin to concern peeking through his professional façade.

I bobbed my head, avoiding his gaze as I shoved down the emotion building behind my eyes at the realization that maybe I didn't know my father all that well after all.

"Tell me about a normal day for your dad. Was he a hands-on kind of guy or more of a delegator?" Ryder pulled a small notepad from his pants pocket and flipped it open.

I shook my head. "Look, clearly I don't know the first thing about my dad, unless you want to know how he took his martini. Dirty, in case that's enough for you to convict him." I tried to keep the sarcasm at bay. I just didn't try very hard.

"Huh," he muttered, stubbled jaw slack for a second like he had more to say, but then he snapped his mouth shut.

"Maybe you should ask Britton," I said. "I'm sure she could tell you everything, down to his morning bathroom ritual," I snapped.

"I did. She said I could talk to her lawyer."

"Huh," I mocked.

He raised an eyebrow, letting me know the jab was not lost on me.

"Why are you asking about his daily habits?" I asked. "I'm pretty sure that's irrelevant now that he's gone."

"It's very relevant in a murder investigation."

"Murder." There it was. It was one thing to suspect it, but to hear it confirmed by Mr. Fed created an aching sensation in my chest that I hadn't expected.

"The routine tox-screen came back with elevated levels of several chemical compounds. They're running a more intensive test now to narrow down the exact cause of death."

"Compounds?" I asked. "You mean, poison?" I felt myself going lightheaded.

Ryder placed a hand on my arm. "Are you sure you're okay? Do you need to sit down?"

I shook my head emphatically. "DynoDrink."

"Excuse me?" Detective Ryder took a step back, his eyebrows drawn downward.

"Britton is positive someone poisoned my dad's health shake mix. DynoDrink." I pointed to Rafe's poster on the side of the slot machine closest to us. He was smiling brightly, holding a can of the powder in one arm and popping a massive bicep with the other.

"Why does she think that?" he asked.

"She saved it. Says it even smells different." I paused. "But anyone had access to it, not just Britton," I added.

"Right." He didn't sound convinced. "In any case, it shouldn't be too hard to get a warrant for testing," he said, maybe more to himself than me as he pulled out his cell and began dialing numbers.

Almost as an afterthought he looked back at me as he lifted the phone to his ear. "You okay?" he asked again.

I nodded. "Just peachy." I was really going to have to work on that sarcasm thing.

But Ryder didn't seem to notice, turning his attention to whomever was on the other end of his call.

I watched his retreating back, telling myself the revelation that Britton was, in fact, right about my dad's death didn't change anything. He was still gone, Britton was still alone, and I was still counting down the days until I could get back to my real life and out of this ridiculous casino.

Speaking of which...there was still the matter of Mr. Price.

Shoving my emotions down, I turned my attention back to the tables. I held nothing back as I grilled each dealer between hands, but no one remembered anything about Mr. Carvell's companion. Nothing specific, anyway. Average height, average looks. He was blond to a couple of dealers, brunette to the next. He hadn't won big, hadn't lost big. No reason for anyone to remember him among the sea of faces they saw each day. No one had seen anything.

I leaned back against an empty table, completely ready to admit defeat and go drown my sorrows in that hot tub Britton had mentioned.

But when I tilted my head back for an overly dramatic sigh, I spied the cameras. The same cameras I had just pointed out to Suit Man that were dedicated to each table. And I felt my defeat giving way to a glimpse of hope.

*Someone* had seen something.

# CHAPTER EIGHT

———

The elevator opened on the second floor, and I was immediately greeted by two very large guys in dark suits with quite distinct bulges at their sides. The larger of the two stepped forward as the doors shut behind me.

"This isn't a floor for patrons, ma'am." He reached around me and pushed the down arrow.

"I'm not a patron, I'm—"

But he didn't give me a chance to finish, instead gently nudging me back into the elevator and adding, "Have a nice stay at the Royal Palace Casino."

I opened my mouth to protest, but the doors slid shut before I could get out more than a squeak. I rode back down to the lobby feeling my face flush and exited to regroup. After giving myself a good mental pep-talk, I pushed the up button again.

When the doors opened again, the guard rolled his eyes. "Ma'am," he started.

But this time I was not letting him run the conversation.

I stepped out and stood directly in front of him, tilting my head back to make eye contact instead of addressing his belly button. "Do you know who I am?"

"Yes, Ms. King. Mr. Malone told us you'd be coming and to direct you back to the floor or to your room. Shall I push the up arrow instead?" He reached around me again, but I swatted his hand away.

I snapped my hands to my hips and narrowed my gaze. "Did he also tell you that I am currently the owner of this casino?" I huffed, channeling my inner bitch with all my might. "Which makes me your boss."

His eyes widened a bit, but little else changed. "I'll see if Mr. Malone is available to speak with you." He lifted a hand to his ear and spoke into his sleeve like I'd seen Secret Service do in TV. A moment later, Alfie filled the hallway behind him.

"Ms. King, is there something I can help you with?" He widened his stance and crossed his arms over his broad chest.

I opened my mouth, but he didn't even give me a chance to finish inhaling, let alone speak.

"If this is about the dispute near the poker tables, I can assure you that we are taking care of the matter. We thank you for your assistance. Take the day to explore the amenities we have to offer. There is a wonderful spa and fitness center on site. My guys will take care of..."

"I'm not here on vacation," I interrupted. "And, as you very well know, this isn't my first visit. I know where the *amenities* are."

"Wonderful. Then why are you here?" he asked, leveling his gaze at me.

"I need to see the video footage from the day Mr. Carvell said he met Mr. Price."

Alfie's jaw clenched. I watched as his chest rose slowly. He let out a deliberate breath before speaking. "We are handling that as well. Might I suggest you busy yourself browsing some of the local craft shows for pieces for your shop back home?"

"I curate a fine art gallery," I said, hearing the defensive tone in my own voice. "I acquire high-end—"

"Same thing," he cut me off. "Mind your own business, and we'll mind ours." He waved a dismissive hand toward me and turned to go back into the bowels of the security floor.

I pushed past the guards easily now that the fight wasn't theirs, and grabbed Alfie's arm. "For the next nine days, the casino *is* my business. I'm not going off on some souvenir hunt, and I'm not leaving this floor, either."

Alfie growled. "You've always been a stubborn broad."

"That's it. You're fired for gender insensitivity."

Alfie smirked, knowing as well as I did it was a hollow threat. But it got the point across.

"Fine. Always a pleasure to work with such a *determined woman*," he amended. Then he pointed to a chair and barked, "Sit. I'll cue up the footage."

I flopped into the cushy leather desk chair and absorbed my surroundings as Alfie marched down the hallway. The security floor was cordoned off only by glass partitions, giving it an open, almost never-ending feel. Dark furnishings spotted each office space. Enormous screens were mounted at eye level throughout the area with random shots of the casino floor and hallway footage playing on each one. Men and women shuffled by me with arms full of files, the occasional person smiling or nodding. The whole area had a choreographed chaos feel to it.

Alfie cleared his throat, standing in the hall to my left. Nothing else, just a cough. And a pair of blank eyes that could have been plotting my death or envisioning the tall scotch he'd be downing after work.

I followed him to the end of the corridor. A cinderblock wall lined one end of the room, the other walls made of glass. Instead of the posh furnishings, like the offices we'd passed, this one had only a tiny metal desk and an old upholstered chair. I almost had to squint to see the tiny twelve inch screen in front of me as I sat down.

"Really?" I probed. "This is the best you can offer me?"

"Our resources are limited, Ms. King. All of my people are busy," he said. Though, true to his word, Alfie had queued up the poker tables on the day before Carvell's cash went missing.

"I'm not sure what you think you'll find," he said, reluctantly showing me how to fast-forward and pause. "We've already been through this footage. Obviously," he added, rubbing in the fact that he was a professional and I was not.

I shrugged. "Maybe I'll see something you missed."

He snorted, but didn't comment, instead leaving me alone in my makeshift office with the small TV. I settled in, watching for Mr. Carvell and hopefully getting a glance at the elusive Mr. Price. Minutes of mind numbing footage of casino tables, cards, and players, all covered in a smoky haze, quickly turned into hours. I forced myself to concentrate on the computer screen, but my mind kept wandering to the conversation I'd had with Agent Ryder.

If I was moving down his suspect list any it was only because he was realizing the same thing I was—that what I knew about my father could barely fill a Post-it. Never mind the fact that I'd been miles away when my father had been poisoned; I'd been in the small minority of people who didn't even know about his health kick.

Lost in what-ifs, regret, and endless poker games, I was almost relieved to see my mom's number pop up on my cell phone.

Almost.

"Hi, Mom, I was just about to call you."

"It's not nice to lie to your mother," she told me.

"Well, I was planning to call you soon. I know you were expecting me home yesterday."

"Please tell me you've at least had enough common sense to stay at a quaint rental cabin, since you obviously don't have enough sense to just walk away from that awful town."

My mother, God love her, was not a fan of anything even remotely associated with my father, least of all the casino. If I hadn't watched the wedding video my dad had kept tucked away, I'd probably have a hard time believing they'd ever really been in love. Mom and Dad were polar opposites who had been co-existing under the delusion they could ground one another in their perspective worlds. Mom was the tree hugging, earth saving, nature lover, spending any free time in the mountains; Dad was the luxury living, indoor dwelling, excess lover, obviously spending his spare time in the lounge. The harmony lasted until I was about two years old and couldn't fall asleep without the curtains open, the flashing neon of the strip as my night light. According to my mother, that's when I was officially corrupted. She'd been fighting the good fight with me ever since.

"Mom, I've got some things to tend to before I can come home." I swallowed past the lie I really wanted to tell and blurted, "Dad left me the casino, and I have to wait until the board of directors' meeting in a week and a half. Then I can split my shares between the other members and come home. Please feed Jack." I inhaled a deep breath and let it out slowly, so glad to have that out in the open with her.

Gasping and sputtering was the only reply I got. I waited for a few minutes in case she suddenly became able to form a sentence. No dice.

I continued, "It's not like I'm staying, Mom. I can't leave right now or the casino might fold."

"Good riddance to bad rubbish," she spat.

"Dad spent his whole life building this…"

"Your father is dead," she interjected, her tone dismissive, as though she were telling a stranger.

"This is the least I can do for him," I murmured. "And please don't let my cat starve."

Mom heaved a sigh into the phone. "I'm sorry. You are doing the right thing. I'm proud of you. And you know I'd never let anything happen to Captain Jack."

*Yes, I named my cat after one of super-hot Johnny Depp's characters. Doesn't everyone?* I really did miss that little fur ball.

"Thanks, Mom. Love you."

"I love you, too, sweetheart. Please keep me updated and be careful."

"Always."

After exchanging good-byes, I put the phone in my pocket, turning my attention back to the monotony. The organized turmoil on the security floor kicked up a notch with the afternoon shift change. The smells of hot pockets and lean cuisine replaced the scent of coffee coming from the break room. Extra bodies appeared in the office to watch the casino floor as the gambling crowd multiplied.

One of the new shift appeared in my doorway, offering a smile. "Hi." His face was tinged red as he stared at his finger tracing the rim of the coffee mug clenched in his hand.

I gave him a wave. "Hi."

"Tessie King, right?" he asked.

I nodded. "The one and only."

He stuck a hand out. "Maverick."

I shook it, raising an eyebrow his way. "Really?"

His cheeks went a shade redder. "No, but we all go by nicknames up here. Breaks up the monotony."

I nodded, knowing firsthand how important that could become after days of this. "Nice idea." I paused. "I have to ask, what's Alfie's nickname?"

Maverick's face broke into a wicked grin. "The guys call him Napoleon."

I covered a very unladylike snort.

"But, shhh," he told me, putting a finger to his lips. "Don't tell Alfie."

I made a zipping-my-lips-shut-and-throwing-away-the-key motion.

"Any luck?" he asked, gesturing to my screen.

I rubbed my temples and exhaled slowly. "Nope, I'm afraid not."

"Well, we have the latest in facial recognition software, so if you didn't find him, he wasn't here," he replied confidently as he turned to leave.

"Wait, facial recognition?" Adrenaline flooded my body along with anger and a few thoughts of revenge. Alfie could have mentioned that.

"Sure." He set his cup on my desk and walked around beside me. After giving him Mr. Carvell's room number, Maverick was able to catch a clear image of him leaving his room the morning he checked in. The program then sped into action and popped up a picture every time he was recognized anywhere in the casino. Ten minutes later, we got a hit on a very nice looking younger guy in an Armani suit who spent a *lot* of time chatting up Mr. Carvell at the tables.

"Bingo!" I shouted.

Maverick straightened beside me, partly at my words and partly because Alfie was suddenly filling my doorway, glaring at me.

I stood and broke into an exaggerated smile. "Hey, Alfie, did you know you have facial recognition software here? I really would have thought the head of security would know about this kind of stuff."

Alfie just grunted.

I turned to Maverick. "Can you be a peach and print that picture for me?"

He looked back and forth between us until Alfie finally flinched in the direction of the office next door, and Maverick took off. Within a few minutes he was back, placing the picture of the infamous Mr. Price in my hand.

Beaming, and feeling extremely pleased with myself, I announced, "Thank you so much," as I pranced up the hall toward the exit.

But Alfie was a step behind me. "Just what do you plan to do with that?"

"I plan to catch Mr. Price."

"I don't know who you think you are—" he started. But he was cut off as his phone jingled to life. Reluctantly, he turned his attention to the speaker, barking out a, "Malone."

I watched as his features morphed from frustration at having me invade his personal domain to shock to an absolute stone poker face. Which scared me even more than any emotion he might have displayed.

"What?" I asked, dread building in my stomach as he hung up.

"That was the concierge desk," he ground out, leveling his stony gaze directly at me. "Seems something you might be interested in has been stolen from the safe."

# CHAPTER NINE

———

One floor. The damned supersonic elevator was only going down one floor, but it seemed to take an hour. Alfie, along with one of the guards in suits and three other security personnel had shoved me into the elevator, the same matching blank expression on all five faces. Alfie would neither confirm nor deny my suspicions of what was missing from the safe. I'd already asked him three times, and all I got in return was a clenched jaw and squinty eyes. When the elevator stopped, I squeezed through the partially opened doors and darted to the front desk. I had really hoped Tate would be working, so I'd have an ally. No such luck.

"Thank you for choosing The Royal Palace for your Lake Tahoe stay. My name is Alicia, and I'll be checking you in today," an energetic brunette bubbled in his place. Though her expression turned from pert to one of fear and concern as she spied our little group approaching.

"Buzz us through," Alfie barked as he walked up beside me.

Her rounded eyes never left his narrowed ones as her shaky hand slid under the counter. The door creaked open, and Alfie stepped in front of the group, taking the lead. I felt as though I was being led to my last meal as the security team corralled me through the door. My worst fears were confirmed when I saw Mrs. Ditmeyer standing there, arms crossed firmly over her bedazzled, leopard-print bosom.

Her arm shot out, an accusatory finger pointed mere inches from my nose. "You."

"But, I... he," I sputtered, pointing my finger at the very guard who'd helped me lock up the necklace.

Mrs. Ditmeyer gave me the same up and down scan she had when we'd first met, punctuating it with a quiet snort of disgust. "I don't need excuses or passing the blame. I need my necklace. Now!"

I glanced around the room at the inquisitive faces, all looking at me for answers.

"I put it in the safe." My words sounded shaky even to my own ears.

"You closed the door?" Alfie asked.

"Yes, of course."

"You locked it?" He took a step toward me, his eyes scanning my face.

"Yes," I repeated.

"And you're sure it latched? And it was secure?" He now stood directly in front of me.

"Yes?"

Alfie narrowed his gaze.

"I mean, yes, definitely sure. Very." And I was. "At least ninety-five percent." I tilted my chin, nodding to add confidence to my statement.

Alfie waved an arm toward his minions, and they scattered from the vault, including the guard. I attempted to follow suit, but he caught my collar in his iron grip.

"Mrs. Ditmeyer," Alfie implored, "Please allow my team a chance to look into this travesty. In the meantime, your room and all of your meals are on the house." He pulled her chubby fingers into his free hand and planted a light kiss on her knuckles.

With eyelashes fluttering fast enough to stir a breeze, she purred, "Alfonso, you sweet talker, I'll look forward to your call."

After releasing my shirt, he escorted her to the exit of the vault, filling the door, undoubtedly to prevent my escape. "Schedule yourself a massage and have them bill me," he cooed in her direction, as he watched her disappear into the crowd.

Then he turned to me. His smooth-talking façade dropping, his menacing face quickly replacing it as he closed the door behind him. "Ninety-five percent?"

"Look, the guard actually put the necklace in the box, but I watched him lock it. That's why I gave myself five percent wiggle room."

His eyes narrowed, a small vein in his neck throbbing. "You never leave any room for doubt in a customer's mind. Ever," his voice boomed. "Nine more days," he whispered as he cracked each of his knuckles and studied his shoes intently. "Well, I'm sure a lesson was learned today, at least. By someone. We'll have to write it off as negligence." His gaze narrowed on me.

I felt like I had been hurled back in time, standing before the elementary school principal after socking Alison Daley when she called me a freckle-faced fatty. Small, insignificant, and regretting ever having set foot in this place. I took a deep breath and squared my shoulders, telling myself I was not at fault here no matter how much Alfie's steely gaze tried to tell me I was.

"This was not negligence. It was theft."

That vein throbbed double time. "It was in our hotel safe. There's no way someone could have broken in here."

"'Someone?' No. An employee, yes."

He took a step toward me. "Just what are you implying, Ms. King?"

I felt my confidence waiver, but I was in full throttle now. "What you must already know. Someone inside the casino stole from Carvell, and I'd bet money the same person took the necklace, too."

Alfie froze, his face a perfect poker-playing blank. Then he shook his head as if deciding I wasn't worth it. "Insurance will cover the necklace. Stintner's already filling out the paperwork."

"We should be stopping the thefts, not just sending them to our attorney to write off as a cost of doing business." I inched forward, jutting my gaze up to meet his. "Any successful business is about people, not just numbers. Carvell was upset enough to leave. I'm willing to bet the Toilet Tissue Queen won't take the news that she's not getting that necklace back any better. Why won't you get someone in here to investigate?"

"We are investigating."

"I mean the police."

That vein pulsed so hard I thought it might pop as Alfie took another step toward me, the scent of stale cigars permeating my nostrils. "Well, this one falls on you, boss. You want a cop breathing down your neck during your short stint with the casino?"

"Uh, that would be the guard's neck, not mine." I pointed behind me like he was there.

"That guard did not take that necklace. If someone did swipe the necklace, it was someone way above his pay-grade. It takes more than one person to open that door," he said, gesturing behind him. "There's no sign of forced entry, so the finger will point back to you, sweetheart. I'm not going to let that kind of heat from the cops cripple your father's empire because you *think* you saw the guard lock the box."

"First off," I shouted, gaining steam, "I'm not your sweetheart. Secondly, I don't want my father's empire crippled any more than you do. It's just too much of a coincidence this happened so quickly after the theft in Carvell's room. They have to be related."

Alfie shook his head. "The M.O. is totally different than the others."

I froze. "*Others*? As in, plural?" I took a step back. "That's what the secret handshake look between you and the other security guy was all about in Carvell's room." I tried to reign in my spiral of emotions, but it was no use. I paced the small area. "I knew there was something more going on. What kind of numbers are we talking here?"

Alfie growled, staring daggers at me for a few seconds before shaking his head. "Three others in the past two months. All of them from room safes, all secure with no forced entry. Carvell and another guy were buy-ins to a private high-stakes game."

I waited patiently for the rest of the stats. Okay, I waited for a couple of seconds before prodding him along. "And the other two?"

Alfie shrugged his huge shoulders. "The guys wouldn't say. But, considering we don't exactly condone that sort of thing, it's not out of the question that they were holding out on us."

"And now the necklace is missing." My mind was spinning with possibilities of how the robberies fit together. It had to be more than mere coincidence.

"The necklace is a fluke. We've had other stuff turn up missing and have had people with sticky fingers in the past. You need to go join Mrs. Ditmeyer at the spa and butt out." He beat on the steel door, and it was immediately opened.

My cell phone chirped to life, saving Alfie from the not so nice words poised on my tongue. I followed Alfie through the door and out into the lobby, watching Rafe's number appear on my screen as I pulled the phone from my pocket.

"Hey," I answered, making a conscious effort to keep the lingering anger from my conversation with Alfie out of my voice.

"Hey, yourself. Ready to hit the mountain?"

Crap. In all of the excitement, I'd forgotten all about my promise to Rafe. While playing ski bum was the last thing on my to-do list, I had to admit that working my anger out through some physical activity might not be a bad thing. Not to mention getting away from the casino for a couple of hours. "Um, I didn't really pack for snowboarding. I don't even have gloves." I looked around at the maze of hallways wondering which one took me to the pro shop.

"No worries. You're about the same size as my manager. Come on up to my room. I've got some of her stuff stashed here."

While borrowing the Barbie's gear ranked up there with eating glass, I was left with little choice. Within a few minutes, I was standing at his door. I took a big gulp of air, telling Teen-me that she was to stay firmly behind this time. This was an outing for the adults. The ones who were just two friends, doing a little snowboarding together. No giggling, no crushing, no heart-doodling.

I knocked, and the door was immediately opened by Rafe, who was still buttoning up his shirt. His chest was tanned, chiseled, and smooth. I'm pleased to report that even in the face of the hormone rush, I was able to keep Teen-me from jumping him on the spot. Just call me Ms. Restraint.

He raised a brow. "Everything okay?"

"Huh? Yeah, why?" I forced myself to look at anything but him, glancing around his pristine suite. It was a copy of mine, though flipped to the mirror image. I wasn't sure what I had expected, but it was clear this was just a landing pad for Rafe, the room void of any personal touches. In fact, the only things not tidily tucked away by housekeeping were his gear and an awful, bright pink blob lying on his sofa I prayed wasn't what I thought it was.

"You stand goofy, right?" he asked.

I took a moment to review boarding lingo, remembering that goofy meant right foot forward, regular meant left. I nodded.

"That's what I thought I remembered. So does Sasha. She's got a board stashed with my stuff at the lodge. She's about your height and weight, so it should work."

I took that as a supreme compliment, considering that in the poster I'd seen she'd looked at least two dress sizes smaller than I was. But if you took into account the extra weight from her inflated boobs, he might be close to right.

"We might have to rent you boots, but Sasha's coat and ski pants should fit you just fine." He motioned toward the pink puff.

Damn. On the flip side, there'd be no problem finding me in an avalanche.

I forced a smile to my face and unfolded the mound. Yep, the pants matched the pink puff of a jacket. Goody. I stepped into the bathroom and swapped my skirt out a pair of stretch pants (in pink, too, of course), a form-fitting top and the pink marshmallow man outfit. The pants were a little snug, but nothing I couldn't move in. But when I put on the coat, I had plenty of extra room in the chest area. Of course I did.

I came out to see Rafe in his black gear covered in endorsement patches, a lopsided grin tugging at his lips.

"What?" I asked.

"You should wear pink more often," he said, sending me one of his groupie-swooning smiles. "You look cute in it."

The hot snowboarder called me cute. Teen-me just about died.

"Let's hit the powder," he said, grabbing me by the hand and propelling me to the elevator. We hit the lobby and made our way out into the parking area without Rafe even acknowledging anyone who tried to stop us. Fans seemed to have tag-teamed themselves in our path, but he didn't seem to notice. I'm sure I was nothing more than a pink blur to everyone. The cool air outside was a welcome relief after being bundled up in the warm hotel.

The walk from the casino to the gondola at Heavenly Ski Resort was just over a block, long enough to be glad when we hit the rustic building, but not so tiring that I was out of breath. I was happy that with Rafe's celebrity status we were able to circumvent the long lift line. We were escorted by the staff around the building, through the back entrance, directly to the gondola. Sitting next to each other on the gondola, I stared out over a deep blanket of snow, real and manufactured. We rose past crags and valleys as we traveled up the pine speckled mountainside. I hadn't realized until that moment how very much I'd missed it all: the cool bite of the air, the starkness of a fresh blanket of snow, the excitement building as you rode the smooth lift to the peak.

"So, I looked up your gallery online," Rafe said, breaking into my thoughts.

"My artists are awesome, aren't they?" I said, unable to help the bit of pride in my voice.

He turned his green eyes toward me. "They were good," he said, though I detected a note of hesitation in his voice.

"But?" I asked, jumping on it.

"But I didn't see anything from you."

"Me?" I laughed. "God, no. I'm not an artist. I'm a curator."

"Why did you settle for that?"

"I... I didn't *settle*," I sputtered, suddenly feeling like I had to defend myself.

"You didn't go to art school to buy other people's stuff. You went to paint."

Luckily I was saved from having to answer that as the gondola jerked to a stop, cutting our conversation short. We made our way out the door and across the well-traveled snowy paths. People flocked around Tamarack Lodge, a log cabin style spot that sold $5 hot cocoa and massively overpriced beer. Some people slid around on skis, others tramped in furry boots, all of them wearing sunglasses to cut the glare off the brilliantly white snow.

We made our way to Rafe's private locker, where he produced a pair of boards—his black and covered in more endorsements, mine baby pink. I was really starting to hate Sasha. We found an empty bench, and Rafe grabbed a small screwdriver attached to the side of it to adjust my bindings. While he did, I breathed in the clean, crisp air and couldn't help the sigh that escaped me when I exhaled.

I heard Rafe chuckle beside me.

"What?"

He shrugged. "Nothing. Breathe it in, girl."

"Hey, I've been inhaling that city crap for years. This stuff is… invigorating. Intoxicating. It's orgasmic," I blurted out. Then instantly wished I had a verbal delete key.

Rafe's hearty laugh echoed between the peaks. "Honey, you've been dating the wrong guys." Then he winked at me.

Oh, boy. Was he flirting with me? Teen-me blushed so hard her cheeks felt like mini-heaters. And Adult-me got warm in places distinctly more R-rated.

Several of the boarders around us turned at the sound of Rafe's voice, then started whispering and pointing as they recognized him. He grabbed my hand again, tugging me to the Tamarack Express lift before they could descend upon us.

Luckily the lifties let us line-jump again, escorting us to the front where we quickly jumped onto an open chair on the lift. Climbing up a steeper part of the enormous mountain, the colder air even permeated my pink fluff.

As we slid off the chair and strapped our boards on, a knot of anticipation and a teeny bit of fear formed in my gut. It had been a while since I'd been on a board, not to mention that I was getting ready to hurl myself down a gigantic mountain with the area's reigning champ. I'd obviously not thought the whole thing through when I agreed.

But Rafe didn't give me much chance to express my concern, and he shouted, "Race you!" and took off like a shot down the hill.

I swallowed back my pride and pushed off behind him.

Rafe took a commanding lead, glancing back over his shoulder on occasion. I surprised myself with moves I hadn't used in years, even gaining on him a few times. I followed Rafe from slope to lift several times, knowing he was more familiar with the mountain than any trained rescue worker in the area. I had to admit, it felt good to just relax and enjoy myself. Nothing mattered for those few hours but the snow, the amazing mountain scenery, and the view of the tight little butt I followed.

Until the sun started disappearing behind the peak.

Shortly after, we found ourselves back at Tamarack Lodge and the gondola that would take us to Heavenly Village.

And reality.

As I gave back my borrow gear and stashed the now much too-warm jacket in Rafe's locker, I was torn between willing the sun back into the sky and knowing how sore my muscles would already be the next day. The cable car wrenched us back down the mountain, and I watched the remaining sunbeams twinkling on the snow. Rafe's voice tugged me from my reverie.

"So, when was the last time you painted something?"

I waved a dismissive hand toward him and looked back out the window.

"Seriously," he insisted, grabbing my chin in his gloved hand, turning my face back toward his.

I got lost in his emerald green eyes. I mean, *completely* lost myself for a while. I felt my face flush warm in the cool air as I struggled to remember the question. "I-I don't know. A while I guess. I'm just... not that good."

"I thought you were great." His face was somber, serious, and I was suddenly very aware of how close we were to one another. He still held my chin, my face turned upward toward his. Time froze as my eyes locked on his lips. He leaned toward me and his breath brushed my cheek. I was 90% sure he was going to kiss me when our car slowed, the liftie holding a hand to help me out.

Timing.

The end-of-day crowd bustled through Heavenly Village, dragging us along with them back toward the casino. As we walked through slush piled streets back to the Royal Palace, I purposefully avoided eye contact with Rafe, almost afraid it might make me ask about the almost-kiss.

As we rounded the circle drive of the casino, I noticed that local news vans filled most of the space.

Rafe sighed. "I'm sure they want to find out how the snow was today. Do you want a little free publicity? I can plug the casino and you as the new owner. They don't have to know its temporary."

I shook my head emphatically. "No, I think that's best left on a need-to-know basis for now."

"Your call." He bared his teeth at me, giving me his killer smile. "My fans await, then."

He raised a hand as we approached the vans, calling out to the crowd, "Hey, it's good to see you all!"

Heads jerked our way, eyes bouncing from Rafe to me, then back again.

Finally one of the women wearing a Channel Four logo jacket shoved a microphone at Rafe and asked, "What do you think about the allegations that Tessie King killed her father?"

# CHAPTER TEN

I stood shaking beside Rafe as the elevator rose, my mind trying to digest what was happening. Had someone alerted the media that I was a suspect? Had that someone been Ryder? He seemed like he'd believed me about the DynoDrink, but then again, wasn't bluffing part of his job?

"You okay?" Rafe asked, squinting down at me.

I nodded, though it was a bald-faced lie.

I'd never been so glad to have a man take charge of a situation in my life. After the reporters surrounded us, Rafe tucked me under his arm and shoved through the crowd, all while screaming, "No comment!" Cameras clicked and news teams yelled louder and louder, trying to be heard over the others. After a failed attempt to take refuge in my room, outside which another microphone toting blabbermouth was camped, I'd settled on the penthouse.

But as the elevator doors opened, I saw that a very different crowd gathered there. The local police, which was only slightly better.

"What's going on?" Rafe demanded of the officer nearest the door.

I watched recognition wash over the officer's eyes as he darted over to us, though his expression remained impassive. "I'm sorry, Mr. Lorenzo. This is a crime scene, and the details cannot be discussed."

Stepping from behind Rafe's protective presence, I announced, "This is my casino, which makes this my business."

"Ah, Ms. King." The officer's face brightened a bit. "Mrs. King has been asking for you."

Rafe tried to follow behind me as the officer led me in, but the guy instantly put his hand out to block Rafe's path.

"I'm afraid that Ra…Mr. Lorenzo will have to wait here."

"That's bullsh—" he started.

"It's okay," I quickly jumped in before Rafe's temper had any more time to simmer. Antagonizing the police was not going to help my situation with the media any. Or his, for that matter.

Rafe looked like he wanted to say more, but he shut his mouth with a click. Instead, he reached out and tucked a strand of damp hair behind my ear. "You sure?" he asked.

I nodded, doing my best convincing face.

"Don't worry about the reporters. I'm sure Alfie will chase them out soon enough," he told me. "I'll call you later."

I grinned up at him. "Thanks. For everything."

He winked at me, then turned and hit the down arrow. I watched him disappear behind the polished silver doors before following the officer into the hot mess that was now the penthouse.

Kitchen drawers lay on the floor, their contents scattered on the imported marble tile. Furniture cushions and pillows had been tossed around haphazardly, leaving the chairs and couch bare. Dozens of plainclothes detectives and uniformed officers milled around, chatting amongst themselves as they poked and prodded every inch of the place. While the penthouse looked like a tornado had hit, it wasn't until I saw one officer start manhandling the Vermeer that I snapped.

I opened my mouth to yell, but Britton's voice rang above the chaos first. "Be careful with that! It's an original!" She charged through the crowd and swatted the man's gloved hands. Wide eyed, he glanced down at the tiny, pissed-off blonde.

Running to her side, I escorted her away before the man's shock wore off and he decided she'd assaulted an officer. Though I couldn't help adding as I dragged her away, "She wasn't kidding. Be gentle with that painting."

Britton wrapped her arms around me, quivering, clinging as though her life depended on it. "Oh, thank God," she breathed. "Tell them to quit touching everything, please."

"What happened?" I asked.

She shrugged. "I don't know. They just showed up here and said they had a warrant to search everything."

I frowned. Ryder had said he'd look into a warrant for the DynoDrink, but he hadn't mentioned tearing the penthouse apart from top to bottom. I glanced around the penthouse for a glimpse of him, but as far as I could tell, he wasn't there. If he'd been the one to get the warrant, he hadn't stuck around to do the dirty work.

"What in the hell is going on here?"

I spun to find Stintner standing in the doorway.

"I'd like to see a warrant immediately and speak to whoever is in charge," the lawyer's commanding voice roared through the room.

"Oh, thank God," Britton repeated, running to him and doing a repeat of the clinging hug she'd just given me.

The lawyer's eyebrows rose, but he didn't exactly look upset at a hot blonde throwing herself at him. It was probably the most action the old guy'd had in years.

"Tell them to get their grubby hands off my stuff. Some of it's priceless," Britton said, practically wailing the last word.

"Trust me, I intend to," Stintner assured her, grabbing a warrant from one of the officers.

"Did you know the press is downstairs?" I asked Britton while he read the legalese.

She nodded, biting her lower lip, leaving a little void in her ruby lipstick. "It's a nightmare, Tess. What are we going to do?"

I wished I had an answer for that one. "Alfie's on it I suppose?"

Again she nodded. "He called Stintner for me, too."

I looked up at the lawyer, now pointing out a fine legality in the warrant to one of the plainclothes detectives. Clearly Stintner had the situation under control.

"I'm going to find Alfie," I told Britton, hoping he'd be able to clear the hallway at my room first and foremost. "You okay here?"

She took a deep quivering breath and flashed me the most unconvincing smile I'd ever seen. "I'm sure Stintner can handle this."

I gave her a fortifying squeeze on the shoulder before backing toward the door. After the accusations the press had thrown at me, I half expected someone to stop me. But none of the officers even gave me a second look. I slipped into the hallway and pulled out my phone. Though before I could dial the head of security, I noticed I'd had sixteen missed calls in the last hour. Most were from my mother, the others from work and my boss's cell phone. The news of my supposed guilt had obviously hit home.

I thought a really dirty word, then dug through my purse for Agent Ryder's number. I typed it into my phone and texted, *meet me.*

A moment later my phone rang in my hand, his number displaying.

"The media thinks I killed my father," I blurted out as I answered.

"Nice greeting," he observed.

I felt the initial shock I'd experienced at arriving in the middle of a media frenzy all implicating me quickly converting to frustration. "In case you didn't see the hoard of news people demanding my head in the lobby, please note I'm currently incapable of nice!"

"O-kay," he said in a maddeningly calm voice. "What would you like me to do about it?"

"Take my alibi down, interview witnesses to where I was the day my father died, issue a statement saying I am not some monster who killed her own father!" I paced the small hallway, really getting worked up now.

"You want me to take down your alibi now? Last time I asked, you said you didn't remember having one."

"I was sitting at my desk, at work, when I got the message he'd passed. I'd been there since eight." The buzz of inane chatter around me in the gallery as I'd read Britton's text message about my father still rang in my ears. "I'd been home the night before watching TV. Alone, unless you count my cat. The last time I was even in Tahoe was two-and-a-half years ago, and my knowledge of poisons is limited to the fact that you shouldn't lick the seal of envelopes, especially cheap ones, so there's no way I put anything in his health shake, which apparently I'm the only person on the face of the earth who didn't know he drank on a daily basis."

I could have sworn I heard a grin brewing on the other end of the line. "That's some alibi."

"Thank you," I huffed out. Though upon further consideration, I wasn't sure he was complimenting me. "So am I good?"

Ryder cleared his throat. "I've already spoken with both your mother and your boss. They've gone into the local P.D. and filled out statements as to your whereabouts on the day in question."

I paused. "You hauled *my mother* into the police station?!"

"Your mother volunteered to come in," he corrected.

"I'll just bet she did," I mumbled under my breath, imagining the lecture I was going to get the next time I talked to her. "Look, this is all just some big mistake. There's no way I—"

But I was cut off by the elevator dinging and the doors sliding open to reveal Ryder himself. He had on his usual dark slacks and starched dress shirt, but his tie was loosened and his sleeves rolled to his elbows. I blame the transformation from buttoned-down to casual for the slowing of my reflexes as he walked up to me and pulled my phone from my ear. He hit the "off" button, then handed it back. Then looked down at my outfit and raised one eyebrow my way. "Cute."

"It's not mine," I protested against the fluffy pants that were beginning to become way too warm for indoors.

He shrugged. "Too bad. You look good in pink."

I blinked at him trying to decide if he was giving me an actual compliment or just trying to distract me from my tirade.

"Your mother is a very nice woman, by the way," Ryder said, pulling his eyes away from the pink marshmallow-ness of my lower half. "She's worried about you, though. You should call her back."

I shook my head, ignoring the jab at my bad-daughter status. "How'd you know where I was?"

Hands splayed to his sides, he grinned. "I'm a detective."

I narrowed my eyes at him. "Okay, since you have an answer for everything, tell me why the media thinks I killed my father."

His grin disappeared. "Ah, this one will be a bit harder, because I have to delve into the intricate workings of the single brain cell all reporters share."

"Not a fan?"

He shook his head, a frown forming between his brows. "Word of your father's death being changed from natural causes to murder brought them out from under their rocks. Your mother being brought in for questioning didn't help matters. And the fact that you're dating Rafe Lorenzo makes you prime tabloid fodder."

"I'm not dating Rafe," I shot back before I could stop myself.

Ryder raised one questioning eyebrow. "According to the early local news, you spent the day with him. And arrived here arm in arm."

"*His* arm was around me. To protect me from the media," I said. Though even as I was defending my not-dating status to Ryder, I could feel the warmth from Rafe's protective embrace on my shoulders. It wasn't an altogether unpleasant memory.

Ryder nodded, though his expression was unreadable. "Well, that is how rumors get started. And the media spins them into facts."

"Great, so release some statement saying I'm not a killer and set them straight," I told him.

"Should I also let them know you're not dating Lorenzo?"

I felt my eyes narrow again at his mocking tone. "Ha. Ha. Very funny. If you're not the one accused of being a killer!"

He sighed and ran a hand through his hair, making it stick out a little on the sides. It should have looked ridiculous, but somehow it added to the appeal of this new casual side of him. "Look, it's not that simple. Let me put it to you this way: Somewhere in your hometown, a little old lady just happened to be settling in to watch television as the newscast came on. This is probably someone you've known for most of your life, watched you grow up, maybe even babysat you when you were young. Even though you are completely innocent, she is now convinced otherwise and won't stop her pursuit of justice until you are rotting in jail. All thanks to those blood-sucking, fear-mongering, media vultures," he finished, looking almost as worked up as I was now.

"I take it you've had a couple run-ins with the vultures before?"

He nodded. "Oh, yeah." Then he inhaled a deep breath through his nose and released it slowly through his mouth.

"Feel better?" I asked.

"You know?" He cocked his head to the side, a soft smile lighting his stubbled face. "I do, actually."

I took my own deep breath, his shared frustration having diffused some of my anger. "So, why aren't you in there making a mess with those guys?"

"The local police have taken over. It's not my case anymore." He pointed to his loosened tie. "I'm officially off the clock."

I paused. "So, you're not here in an official capacity."

He cocked his head at me. "I suppose not."

"Which means you can talk to me about the case unofficially?"

"Unofficially? Yes," he decided.

I gestured behind myself. "So what are they looking for?"

"My best guess? Whatever poisoned the powdered drink mix."

"So it was the DynoDrink that killed him?"

Ryder nodded. "Ingested about thirty minutes before he died."

Score one for Britton. Apparently she wasn't as dumb as she looked. "So, why are the police searching Britton's stuff? She's the one who told me about the powder. I doubt very seriously she'd implicate herself in a murder."

Agent Ryder arched a brow. "I've been in this line of work for a while. People do what they must to survive." His eyes shifted to the floor. "They have probable cause, or the judge wouldn't have issued a warrant. I read in the file that the penthouse was one of the few areas without surveillance cameras. I'd imagine that's why they started there."

I opened my mouth to protest, but Ryder's phone picked that moment to ring in his pocket.

Glancing at the number, he mumbled, "My boss. I probably should take this," before turning his back to me and answering. I noticed he straightened his tie as he did so. Back to official mode.

I pushed the down arrow as he answered his call and entered the elevator, digesting what he'd just told me. The drink was poisoned in the penthouse. The only place without cameras. I ran the mental list of people who serviced the penthouse and might know what happened that day. One name popped to the top. Ellie Lopez, Tate's mom. I just had to figure out a way through the media circus to find her.

Service elevator!

I pushed on the third floor button before it was too late, jumped out of the elevator, and scurried down the hall toward service elevator at the end. When the doors opened, two of the housekeeping staff stood inside, blocking my way.

A portly older woman pushed the down arrow repeatedly, as her taller counterpart swatted at me through the opening.

"Move back. This isn't the elevator you're looking for."

I shoved my hand between the doors as they started to close. "Yes, it is. My name is Tessie King, and I'm trying to get to the employee lounge to find Ellie Lopez."

The older woman's eyes rounded, and she yanked on the taller woman's sleeve until she bent down. She whispered something, but the only word I could make out was "killer."

I rolled my eyes.

"I did *not* kill my father. And, technically, I'm your boss right now, so don't push it."

She dropped her arms to her sides and stood tall, her eyes still wide. The other woman finally spoke.

"Ellie's on this floor right now." Her hand shot out, pointing at a cleaning cart a few rooms down. "That's her stuff, there."

"Thank you, ladies." I removed my hand from the doors and let them close, but not before hearing the older woman squealing about seeing a real live murderer.

I hated that Agent Ryder was right.

I walked to the cart and peered into the room with the door propped open. "Mrs. Lopez?"

"Yes?" A toilet lid clanged shut, the bathroom door swung open, and out stepped all five feet, one hundred pounds of Ellie Lopez. She was tiny, but I knew for a fact that she did more work than two people twice her size. Her dark hair, shot with streaks of grey, was pulled back in a tight ponytail, her bright blue uniform neatly pressed with a sharp crease running down the front of the slacks. A smile consumed her entire face. "Miss Tess!" She peeled off her rubber gloves and enveloped me in a hug. "Why haven't you come to see me sooner?"

Guilt instantly struck. "Well, it's been kind of a whirlwind since I got here."

She grabbed my shoulders, her face falling somber. "I'm so very sorry about your papá. He was a great man. I owe him so much," she said in heavily accented English. While Tate had grown up in Tahoe, Ellie's roots were in Mexico and, despite the fact she'd been in the country for over twenty years, her voice still held that lilting rhythm from south of the border.

I shook my head. "No, you don't. You're like family."

"You are too sweet." Tears welled in her eyes, but the smile returned to her face.

"Do you have a few minutes?" I asked, gesturing toward the chairs in the room.

"Always, for you."

I sat down across from her and released a heavy sigh. "You take care of the penthouse, right?"

"For most of my career." Her head cocked to the side, brow pinched in confusion.

"Were you working the day my dad..." I swallowed past the lump in my throat.

Ellie grabbed my hand in hers. "Sí, I was there that day."

"Did you know about his latest health drink kick?"

Shaking her head, she giggled. "Of course. Everybody knew. He said he had to be getting in shape to keep up with Britton. He mixed that drink every morning before he and Britton went down to work out and every night before he went to bed."

"Okay," I thought aloud. "If he had one before he went to bed, and was fine, then someone had to mess with the drink powder after that. Or first thing in the morning."

"Wait," Ellie picked up a room service menu and fanned herself, her face flushing pink. "Something was wrong with the drink powder?"

I nodded. "Was there anything suspicious that morning? Anyone come up there who wouldn't normally? Anything out of place?"

"Mr. King locked the penthouse down tighter than Fort Knox at night. I was let in about seven that morning to tidy up, just like always. There was nothing odd when I left at nine."

"You're sure?"

Her head bobbed, eyes wide, her gaze never leaving mine.

That cut the time frame for someone tampering with the powder to between nine and eleven that morning. My phone chirped to life, giving me no time to ponder that thought.

I pulled it from my pocket and showed Ellie the screen sporting Tate's smiling face. "Your son."

She patted my shoulder, snapped her gloves back on, and disappeared back into the bathroom.

"Hey, you," I answered.

"Are you ready to go?"

"Go?" I asked, my brain searching for the "where" that went with that.

"To the Deep Blue," Tate squealed. "Honey, there are some half-dressed men over there who aren't going to ogle themselves!"

Oh boy.

# CHAPTER ELEVEN

———

Luckily Alfie had, in fact, found a way to eradicate the media from the Royal Palace grounds. Probably with a few well placed threats. And security escorts. Possibly a taser or two. Either way, the hallway outside my room was now thankfully clear, leaving me free to ditch my ski clothes, speed through a quick bite to eat from room service, and blast through the fastest shower routine of my life. I'd just dressed and put on my finishing touches of mascara and lip gloss when a noise in the hall caught my attention.

Glancing through the peephole, I saw Tate grinning from ear to ear, struggling with an armload of garment bags.

Opening the door wide, I stood back as he wedged himself and his cargo through sideways. Tate was impeccably groomed, dressed in black skinny pants (well, as skinny as pants got on Tate's generous frame), a charcoal vest, bright purple paisley dress shirt and matching tie. He appeared about twenty pounds lighter, so I was willing to bet he had on some sort of man-Spanx as well.

"Hey, girl," he crooned, laying the bags out carefully on my couch.

I merely raised a brow and nodded toward them. His eyes widened, a guilty expression morphing his perfectly plucked, shaved, and exfoliated face. In our history together, this look has never been good. Tate was a multi-faceted individual, but guilt was rarely allowed in his repertoire.

"Before you freak out," he hedged, hands splayed toward me.

Those words? Also, not a good sign.

"All of these can be returned to the casino boutique." He waved one outstretched hand over the bags while pensively sliding the other down his side, framing his ensemble.

I rubbed my temple, very happy there was alcohol in my near future. "What is all this?"

"Well, while you are, indeed, making a fashion statement…" He paused, scanning me with his critical eye.

"What?" I asked, looking down at my little black dress. While the conservative cut wasn't exactly going to turn any heads at a club, it was about the only option I had for going out. I hadn't exactly packed for a night on the town when I'd left home.

Tate shook his head, then gripped my shoulders with both hands, face sinking into a pity pucker. "Unfortunately, the only statement your fashion is making is, 'hell, no.' Seriously, who wears funeral clothes to a party?"

I considered objecting, but the man did have a point. Instead, I watched him unzip the bags and gently drape each garment over the back of the sofa. Seven dresses total, each amazing, beautiful, stunning even, in different ways.

But so not me.

The first was a white beaded, strapless dress with barely enough material in the skirt to cover the essentials. The second was a blood red floor length evening gown with a slit up the side that wouldn't allow for any privacy. I couldn't help but turn to him and roll my eyes.

"What? It's beautiful."

I nodded in agreement. "For a black tie event and someone with an aversion to panties. I love my panties."

"Touché," he mumbled.

The third dress was gorgeous with dark blue fabric, modest skirt, and cute halter that tied behind the neck. Then I lifted the hanger, and it slid into two pieces. The dress was perfect for a cardio whore addicted to abdominal workouts. Britton would look fabulous in it, but so not me. Not that my stomach was bad, I just didn't much care to display it for all to see.

I discounted the next three dresses on their neon colors alone, which left me with the last dress. Tiny capped sleeves gave way to a fairly low scooped neck, and blue-gray satin that made me smile.

Tate bounced up and down, clapping. "That's the one I figured you'd choose. It actually has you written all over it." He reached in the bottom of the bag, pulling out shoes. Not just any shoes, mind you. *Actual* Christian Louboutins. (So different from the Krisjon Louisbitton version from China that I owned.)

"Size seven, right?" Tate asked.

I squealed like a little girl. Then I glanced at the tag on the dress, sporting a huge designer name with a price to match, and reality slapped me in the face. "I can't afford this. You'll have to send them all back."

"The beauty of this proverbial buffet of clothing is you don't have to pay a dime. All I did was drop your name, and they said I could take whatever I thought you'd like."

"They just let you take all of this?"

"Well, I was escorted by a security guard, but he was cute. Win-win. Just send back what you don't like, and keep what you want, free of charge." He pulled out a receipt with all of the clothing listed, all zeroed out with a place for me to sign. "Evidently, ownership has some major perks."

I flopped on the end of my bed with the silky dress draped across me, staring at the Louboutins Tate still proudly displayed.

He carried the shoes over, tugged me into a sitting position, and sat next to me. "Just wear the outfit for tonight. You can take it back in the morning."

Those words actually made sense and filtered past my mother's long-ago threats of burning anything I brought home from the boutique. It wasn't like I'd be the first woman to ever return a dress after the party she'd bought it for. I'd just make sure I didn't spill anything on it, right?

He enveloped me in a hug and muttered into my hair, "You deserve to be pampered. Let's just pretend we are Cinderella and Prince Charming for the night. I'll even return my clothes tomorrow, if it will make you feel better."

Tilting my head back, I smiled up at him. "I'm pretty sure Cindi and The Charmer wouldn't go watch naked men shake their naughty bits, but I get what you're saying." The distant look in his eyes told me he was either pondering my words or picturing the naked men dancing.

"But," I told him, "if you're going to pull off Prince Charming, you'll have to brush up on your straight guy act."

His spine stiffened, eyes narrowing into a sultry gaze. With a subtle nod of the head, he whispered, "'Sup?"

Giggling, I reached a hand to his soft cheek. "Thanks, Tate."

He winked and waggled his brow. "Now, go put on that cute little dress and work those awesome shoes."

As I stood from the bed, he swatted my butt. I turned at the bathroom door and gave him my best glare. "Don't push your luck, my friend."

"Just practicing my *straight guy*."

"Most of them don't smack with their pinky out, just so you know."

He shoved his hands behind his back. "Noted."

The dress fit perfectly, other than the missing six inches or so at the bottom. It didn't matter how many times I tugged, the hem still hit mid thigh. I slid my feet into the soft leather shoes, and they molded to my toes. I stood, and it felt like I was walking on stilletoed clouds. When I returned to Tate in my room, his mouth dropped open.

"Damn, girl." He grabbed my hands and spun me around. "I've never seen you look more beautiful." Tears welled in his eyes.

"Stop it." I swatted at his arm. "I don't want to have to redo my makeup."

He pushed a little matching leather clamshell purse into my hand. "Now, let's go ogle some hotties."

I felt very self-conscious as we paraded through the lobby, partly because of the dress and partly thanks to the previous media frenzy. Luckily, the news crews were nowhere to be seen, but people still stared, whispered to one another, and pointed in our direction. Tate soaked up the attention, his chest puffing right along with his ego. While I blushed and turned away from most spectators, he nodded and did a Miss America wave. All he needed was a decorated float and a tiara.

The crisp night air swirled around us as we crossed the street to the Deep Blue. The dark concrete building greeted us with flashing blue neon framing every possible angle. A mammoth television screen over the entry displayed a loud, pert blonde woman, touting hotel and casino amenities and drink specials. As we entered, an enormous aquarium nearly filled the open, atrium style lobby. Four stories tall, the tank housed several sleek, grey sharks. Brightly colored schools of fish shifted and darted from their every move.

An awful, unnatural shimmer off to the side caught my attention. Weston was in his signature silk shirt, standing in the VIP section of the casino, surveying the tables as if presiding over his subjects. Tonight's offering was a poison green color. I briefly wondered if he wore them as a way to rival the neon in his casino.

Tate tugged on my arm, pointing toward the growing line to our right, behind a long velvet rope. "We're going to get crap seats. Come on!"

I patted his hand and pulled away. "Save me a place. I have to use the ladies room," I lied, one eye on that shirt, remembering the odd exchange I'd witnessed at the lounge the night before.

After a dramatic sigh, he agreed, "Fine, just hurry up. Text if you can't find me."

Nodding, I moved toward the restrooms. Then as Tate blended into the crowd, I switched course, making my way to the VIP section where I'd spotted Weston. The area consisted of a handful of tables, only distinguished as better than the non-VIP area by their shiny, gold embellishments and pricier buy-ins. The section was raised up a level from the main floor, separated by a waist-height blue neon wall and a rather large man with 'security' stretched across his broad chest. He barred my way as I tried to enter.

"I'm sorry, Miss. This area is reserved for VIP guests only."

I pointed toward the silky glare. "I just need a moment with Mr. Weston."

Mr. Bulky blocked my every move in Weston's direction, his blank facial expression unchanging.

"Please?" I purred, batting my eyelashes, adding a slightly pouted lip and wide doe eyes.

His eyes narrowed, but I watched as he raised an arm to his mouth, chatting into a microphone somewhere in his sleeve. I readied myself to be tossed from the casino, hoping they didn't scuff my new shoes in the process. Instead, I was surprised to see Weston appear at Mr. Bulky's side.

"What can I do for you, Ms. King?" He took a large draw from his cigar and spewed a billow of smoke in my face.

I waved it away, trying to retain my professional composure. Once able to breathe, I asked, "What you can do is tell me what you were doing at the Royal Palace yesterday."

He planted the cigar firmly in the corner of his mouth. "Whatever do you mean?" It bobbed with each word.

"I saw you in the lounge. What was in the envelope you gave to my valet?"

"Oh, that was just a tip for excellent service. Mr. Carvell asked me to deliver it, you know, since he didn't feel safe going over there himself." The cigar-less side of his mouth curled into a malicious grin, matching the rest of his creepiness.

My gaze narrowed on him. "And the other guy?"

Weston blinked at me. "Other guy?"

"Joe Pesci."

Weston's eyebrows formed a "V", a chuckle escaping his mouth. "Honey, I can assure you I have not been cavorting with movie stars."

I shook my head. "Not the *real* Joe Pesci. The look-alike. They guy who grabbed the envelope from you."

Weston's face transformed into a perfect blank. It was the spitting image of every poker player I'd grown up watching at my dad's tables. "I can't imagine who you're talking about."

I had a pretty good idea he knew exactly who I was talking about. And the fact he was lying about it aroused my suspicions all the more.

Frustrated, and fairly certain I would get nothing more from him, I shook my head and turned away.

"By the way, you looked great on the news tonight!" he bellowed over the dinging machines.

I stopped, anger churning inside me. I considered spinning around with a snappy retort but chose to keep walking, instead. Mainly because after the day I'd had, I was fresh out of anything resembling snappy.

By the time I got back to the roped off area outside the show, only a few people milled about. The man running the door waved us away. "Sorry, the show is at capacity."

Already beyond hacked off, I pushed my way to the front, and barked, "My friend is saving a seat for me."

Staring at his clipboard, the doorman rolled his eyes. "At least be creative, sweetheart."

"Sweetheart?" I seethed. "Listen here, douche-nozzle, my name is Tessie King and I—"

But I didn't get any further as his eye popped up from his clipboard, recognition finally dawning in them. "Ms. King. Of course there's room for you. Let me show you to your table."

I had to admit, I could get used to throwing my name around like this.

The club pulsed with DJ mixed tunes, the lights flashing with the beats as we wound through groups of patrons. Heavy red curtains draped in front of the stage matched the rich tablecloths dotting the crowded room. Several spinning disco balls speckled the walls and people with twinkling lights.

Tate bounced from his seat at a small table only two rows from center stage. Always the gentleman, he greeted me with a huge smile, pulled out my chair, and helped me get situated.

He set an apple-tini in front of me and yelled over the music, "Drinks are on me tonight!"

Had I not just passed a sign touting buy one-get one free, I'd have been touched. I gulped the green drink, then signaled the scantily clad waitress with a gesture toward my empty glass. Nodding, she disappeared in the chaotic crowd around the bar.

I glanced around at the sea of women's faces. The occasional bored man blended in, with the exception of a few of Tate's friends, who came screaming toward our table. I found myself very happy for the loud music. They giggled, pointed, and squealed until the waitress returned with two drinks for each of us. Then Tate group-hugged his friends good-bye and sat down. The alcohol induced warmth spread through me as I sipped at my second, releasing some stress from the past few days just in time for the DJ to announce the show.

A sexy male voice hummed over the loud speakers, "Without further ado, give it up for the Deep Blue Male Revue!" The heavy red curtains parted, revealing six men wearing bright yellow raincoats and hats. The song *It's Raining Men* filled the air, as each dancer tossed his hat into the audience. One landed on Tate's lap. Swooning, he clutched the floppy plastic to his chest, squealing at the top of his lungs.

Women rushed the stage, varying in age from barely legal to barely breathing. Makeshift bridal veils covered in condoms and other novelty bachelorette pieces spotted the crowd. I pulled my other drink to my lips, very disappointed to find it empty and unsure if Tate or I had drunk it. With Tate desperately trying to make eye contact with the man who threw the hat, I slid his extra drink toward me. The men teased the crowd, slipping a shoulder out of their coat, flashing their shiny yellow G-string at anyone waving a dollar in their direction, grinding their hips to the beat of the music. They were all chiseled and beautiful, and as cheesy as the setting was, I was having a hard time not enjoying myself.

I blame it on the apple-tini that my mind started to wander, irrationally putting one hot snowboarder with bright green eyes in those raincoat outfits. I had no doubt that his abs rivaled any that were currently gyrating in front of me. I bet he even had those kinds of moves. Athletes were agile like that, right? I felt myself go warm, suddenly imagining those kinds of moves *horizontal*. All of my teen fantasies about Rafe had always ended in an innocent kiss and declaration of undying love. But my rising blood-apple-tini level now had my mind running wild into a very *not* innocent territory about the guy I was *not* dating.

I frowned, memories of the way I'd so vehemently protested to Agent Ryder that I was not coupled with Rafe suddenly invading my pleasant trip to fantasyland. Why had I done that? I mean, so what if the media thought I was with Rafe? Or if Agent Ryder thought it. I mean, it's not like I cared what Ryder thought. It was none of his business who I was or wasn't dating. I'm sure Agent Ryder didn't care. I mean, it's not as if he had any stake in my being single.

Let's face it, between the two of them, those guys ran the bad-boy gamut. Rafe was a dark, devilish playboy. The kind of guy a girl thinks only she can tame. Ryder was a tall, built, mystery man. The kind of guy a girl thinks will open up just for her. Of course, the logical *woman* in me knew both statements were pure crap. Bad boys only led to bad breakups and bad ice cream binges where you spent hours crying to your cat about how you should have known better.

You know, not that this had ever happened to me, personally.

But even as I knew the truth of that situation, I couldn't help my mind sliding over Ryder's tussled look that afternoon. Tie askew, sleeves rolled high enough to show off tanned, toned forearms. Casual had looked good on him, I decided, sipping at my drink again. The way his hair had mussed when his hands ran through it reminded me of how it must look when he rolled out of bed in the morning. I pictured him as the kind of guy who slept in his boxers, bare chest, probably just a light, silk sheet covering his…

Good God, was I picturing Agent Ryder in bed?

I gave myself a mental shake, downing the rest of my drink as I focused on the show.

A few girls got pulled up on stage, and Tate immediately turned a wide-eyed glance toward me, looking like a kid pleading for ice cream.

I shook my head. "Oh, no. No way."

But he ignored me, grabbing my hand and tugging me toward the stage, knocking into several girls standing nearby in the process.

"Sorry," I mouthed. Head spinning, I felt myself being hoisted onto the stage by a dark haired Adonis who immediately wrapped me in his arms, swaying me seductively to the music.

*Carpe Diem, right?*

I had enough alcohol spinning through my system that I tossed caution to the wind and moved along with him to the beat of the music. I was even a little sad when I felt Tate tugging the hem of my dress. His hands gripped my hips, and I fell back into his arms.

His very strong arms.

Sobering quickly, I turned around and, instead of finding my dancer-ogling friend, I looked up into the face of a very befuddled FBI Agent.

Oh damn.

Smoothing my dress back into place, I gave one more tug in a last ditch attempt at those extra few inches from the hem. Not that I had any dignity left to cover. "Agent Ryder," I muttered, looking everywhere but directly at him.

He nodded in my direction, a grin tugging the corner of his mouth. "Ms. King."

I cleared my throat, trying to shove down the image of him in boxers and nothing else, lying on silk sheets that I somehow could *not* shake from my brain now. That's it. I was never drinking apple-tinis again.

"What are you doing here? I thought you were off the case," I said, hoping the dim lighting covered the blush taking over my features.

I looked up to find Tate standing directly behind Agent Ryder, emphatically mouthing the word 'yum'.

Agent Ryder leaned down and said, "I have other interests here."

I glanced back and forth between the male dancers on the stage and him. Obviously hearing Ryder's admission, Tate began dancing behind him, mouthing 'he's mine'.

"Other interests?" I cocked my head at the half-naked men on stage.

Agent Ryder's grin turned to shock. "No!" he said quickly. "Not that kind of interest. I mean, not *here*, here, but here."

Agent Ryder was flustered. Cute. I couldn't help the grin transferring to my face now.

He cleared his throat. "I saw you entering the revue. I followed you in. End of story."

Tate's dancing came to an abrupt halt. Shoulders slumping, his face fell into a pout. I must have been staring, because Agent Ryder turned toward him.

Tate stood tall, nodded at Ryder and muttered, "'Sup?"

I barely resisted the urge to roll my eyes.

After shaking Tate's hand, Ryder faced me again. "This isn't exactly staying out of the public eye."

"Alfie chased the media away," I told him.

"From the *Royal Palace*."

"Oh." It was a good point, and one I hadn't thought of. I looked around the assembled bachelorettes and soccer moms gone wild. While I didn't see any news channel insignias blazoned on their shirts, it wasn't out of the question that those cell phones in their hands were filming me and not the hotties on stage.

"What exactly are you doing here?" I asked, turning the focus back on him.

He shook his head. "It's an official capacity."

"I thought you were off the case."

"Of your father's death, yes."

I waited for him to go on, but he just stared at me. Or, more accurately, at my cleavage. "It's kind of low, right?" I admitted.

He blinked his eyes up to meet mine. "What?"

"The neckline. I know it's too low, but it's not my dress. See, I'm just borrowing it. I don't normally dress like this," I said, tugging my hemline again.

I watched Ryder's Adam's apple bob up and down. "You should. You look..." he paused, his eyes sliding to my hemline. "...great."

I felt my face flush, but before I could respond, Tate—clearly losing interest in the heterosexual Ryder—was grabbing my hand and pulling me toward the stage again.

"Look, fresh meat!" he cried, pointing to a new crop of dancers on stage.

I glanced back over my shoulder, but Ryder was gone, melting into the crowd and taking off on whatever "official" business had brought him here in the first place.

"Oh-em-gee, I'm in love," Tate squealed.

I turned my attention back to the new beefcakes gyrating and grinding to the beat of the pulsing music. My gaze narrowed on the lead dancer's features, a spark of recognition filtering into my foggy brain.

I pushed my way closer to the stage, as he stripped to his G-string, and waited for him to stop shaking his booty. When he turned around, I suddenly knew exactly who he was.

The elusive Mr. Price, in the flesh.

# CHAPTER TWELVE

———

"That's the guy I've been looking for!" I yelled.

"Me, too. He's delish, right?" Tate said, punctuating the statement with a war-whoop holler.

"No. I mean, yes, he's delish. But that's not what I meant. I know him." I pointed my finger in Mr. Price's direction. Then I pulled Tate's head down toward me and spoke directly into his ear. "He was using the name of Mr. Price at the Royal Palace and promised one of our high rollers an exclusive high-stakes game."

"Oh." Tate's eyes got big as the light bulb of recognition went off. "Ohmigosh, Mr. Carvell? This is the guy who stole his cash?"

Nodding, I looked around suspiciously. Like anyone could hear or even cared. Every eye was focused on the dancers. "Maybe. I mean, he's definitely the guy who was setting up the fake game. Whether or not he stole the money..." I trailed off shrugging.

"Maybe he just likes to play poker in his spare time?" Tate said, obviously reluctant to think anything bad about Mr. Hottie.

I flung my hand toward Mr. Price. "That guy was dressed way above his Chippendale dancer pay grade. Armani, Tate, and not the stuff you get at the mall."

"You saw him?"

"I saw him on camera. I spent a mind numbing afternoon going through footage to find the guy our customer said met him at the tables."

Tate's nose scrunched again. "What took so long? I thought we had facial recognition software."

"Oh, we do. That was just something that slipped Alfie's mind," I muttered sarcastically. "Anyway, the guy up there was posing as a high roller with private game connections. My guess is he's working for someone else. His job is to get the target to order in a large amount of cash so someone with access to the rooms can clean out the safe before the supposed poker game."

Tate's lips pursed, and he ran his finger and thumb over an imaginary mustache, deep in thought. "Who would have access to the rooms except..." He paused, then shook his head violently from side to side. "No way. You don't think a casino employee is involved, do you?"

I took a deep breath. "Yeah, I do." I hated saying it out loud, but there it was. As Tate said, who else would have access?

"Honey, I honestly can't imagine any of our employees getting involved in something like that."

As much as I didn't want to imagine it, Alfie had almost confirmed as much. "That's why we have to go talk to him." I gestured toward Mr. Price again. "We need to find out who he's working with."

Tate's eyes lit up like Christmas. "Does that mean we get to go backstage?" he asked, bouncing back and forth from one foot to the other, frantically shaking his hands.

I nodded. "I think we need to." Though I was having a hard time getting as giddy about it as Tate. Hot guys in thongs on stage was one thing. In person, I had a feeling things were a lot less glamorous and a lot more embarrassing.

The song ended and the men filed off stage, Mr. Price leading the way, as new dancers marched on from the other side.

"Now's our chance," I said, nudging Tate.

I barely had the words out before Tate was knocking people out of our way and clearing a path for us.

The backstage door was partly opened, a guy in a black "Security" T-shirt standing near it. Luckily for us, his attention was engaged with a cute little blonde who was currently trying to suck his lips off his face. As the blonde jumped into the guy's arms, straddling his waist, I grabbed Tate's hand and yanked him through the door with me.

Men of all shapes and sizes milled about the open aisles in various stages of undress. I felt my cheeks go warm, resisting the urge to cover my eyes with both hands.

Lighted vanities stocked with makeup lined the walls, racks of clothing filling the center of the room. A few guys with clipboards barked orders as they made their rounds, while a few others dug through the racks and handed out clothing.

I grabbed a rainbow colored G-string from one of the racks, trying to blend in as wardrobe. Tate followed my lead, picking up an abandoned clipboard. Together we roved the room, searching among the faces of the dozens of dancers for Mr. Price. Or, more accurately, *I* searched faces. Tate was having a hard time keeping his eyes above waist-level.

Though I wasn't sure either of us was having a tremendous amount of luck. In the fluorescent lighting and crush of nearly-nude bodies, all the guys blended together. Without the stage spotlight directing my attention to Mr. Price, I was having a hard time picking him out of the crowd.

"Hey, honey, you new?" I heard a voice behind me.

I spun to find a huge, six-foot-four guy in teeny, tiny hot pants standing behind me. Very close behind me.

Instinctively I took a step back.

"Uh, yeah. New."

"Daaaaamn," he said, drawing the word out as his eyes roved my dress from low neckline to high hemline in a way that suddenly made me feel like I needed a shower. "You dress mighty fine for a wardrobe girl."

"Yeah, well, we're upgrading," I mumbled, my eyes darting left and right for Tate. Unfortunately, he was lost in the racks and naked men.

"Oh, that's the kind of upgrade I like," the guy said, taking a step closer.

I tried to take another back, but came up against the wall, suddenly feeling nervous as the Neanderthal closed what little gap existed between us.

I cleared my throat. "Uh, look, I'm just looking for a dancer—"

"You got one, honey," he said, cutting me off.

"No, I mean a specific dancer. He was just on stage?"

Neanderthal's sacchariny sweet smile broadened into a positively lewd leer. "Baby, trust me. When I get done with you, you won't want anyone but me."

I swallowed a lump of fear and revulsion as he pressed himself against me. I was just about to scream bloody murder—not that I had much hope of being heard over the pulsing music from the stage, when a shiny piece of metal slid between us, grazing the guy's throat.

Tate's shaky voice barked, "Let her go, or I will end you."

Neanderthal froze, then took a step back, putting distance between us again.

"That's better," Tate said, his voice cracking only slightly.

The dancer's eyes shot from Tate to what I now noticed was a straight razor right out of a 50's movie. "Dude, I didn't know she was yours." He put his hands up in a surrender motion.

Our little altercation had caught the attention of another dancer, one I recognized as dancing backup to Mr. Price. He was smaller than Neanderthal, but tanner and more toned, wearing a pair of black, tear-away pants and a bowtie at his neck.

"You getting your ass handed to you again, Damien?" the guy asked, a teasing tone in his voice.

Damien grunted, a scowl marring his features. "You're not my type, anyway," he spat in my direction before turning away.

"Yeah, right," the tan guy said. "Anything with a pulse and a pair of tits is your type," he joked. Then he shot me a wink before making his way to a vanity in the center of the room.

I let out a sigh of relief so deep it ruffled my hair. I saw Tate do a mirror image of it.

"You okay, honey?" he asked, his voice as shaky as my legs felt now that the rush of adrenaline was fading.

I nodded. "This dress is dangerous. It's totally going back in the morning."

Tate nodded. "Agreed."

"But, thanks," I told him. "My hero."

He laughed, shaking his own adrenaline rush out of his system as he slipped the razor back into his pants pocket.

I gestured to it. "Since when do you carry a razor?"

Tate grinned. "Hey, a boy's got to have protection. I got it when *Grease* came to town. Cute souvenir and scary accessory all in one."

I couldn't help grinning back. "Only you would carry a weapon from a musical." We giggled together, working the last of the nerves out of our systems.

I glanced over to the vanity in the center of the room where Tan Man was applying one last coat of bronzer to his chest before taking the stage again. "We should go thank him, too."

Tate followed me to the table where I extended my hand toward the guy. "Thanks for having our backs," I said.

"Hey, no sweat," he said, wiping the bronzer on a towel before shaking my hand. "Damien's a dick. You've got to watch out for guys like him. I'm pretty sure he's just trying to make up for a pocket pinkie." He punctuated his statement with a smile and a wink.

Then he looked past me, and his smile widened. "Who's your friend?"

"This is Tate." I waved over my shoulder.

Tan Man practically nudged me out of the way to take Tate's hand in his. "Well, hello Tate. I'm Michael James." He raised Tate's knuckles to his lips in a soft kiss. Their gazes met, and I'm pretty sure Tate almost fainted, his lashes fluttering faster than hummingbird wings.

"Hi," Tate squeaked while fanning himself with his free hand.

"Do you have a last name, Tate?"

"Um, yes." His eyes widened, and the fanning became frantic.

"And it is?"

"Uh..."

"Lopez," I supplied for my friend, whose hormones had obviously caused a short circuit between his brain and lips.

"Yes! That's my name." The fanning stopped, but his head kept bobbing his acknowledgement.

I stifled a laugh at his *smooth* moves. But if Michael noticed, he didn't say anything. Instead he just continued staring at Tate as if he were a brand new toy he just couldn't wait to play with.

"Uh, listen, we're looking for a...friend," I cut into the hook-up moment. "He was dancing the lead in that number you guys just did out there." I gestured toward the stage door.

"Brad?" Michael asked.

"That's him. Our friend Brad," I said, hoping I sounded convincing. "Is he around?"

But Michael shook his head. "He had to skate. Said something about another gig. Must have been late because he left in a big hurry."

"Another dancing job?" I asked, though I feared that "gig" would be portraying Mr. Price somewhere.

"No, he's an actor. He gets bit parts around town and in Reno. We both do."

"You're an actor?" Tate breathed in a seductive voice that could rival Marilyn Monroe any day.

Michael smiled and nodded. "I am. This dancing stuff just pays the bill between gigs. But I've got an audition for a soap in Reno next week."

"Ohmigod, a soap star," Tate said, practically swooning as he gasped air in and out.

"Wait, they film soap operas in Reno?" I couldn't help but ask. It was the nearest big city, but Hollywood it was not.

Michael nodded. "It's a Spanish soap, but the part is great. I play the Latin lover of the lady of the house whose husband is in a coma."

"The Latin lover," Tate breathed heavily, eyes glazing over.

He was going to start hyperventilating at this rate.

"Uh, do you happen to have Brad's phone number?" I asked.

If Michael thought it was odd that Brad's "friend" didn't know his number, he didn't register it, instead soaking up Tate's adoring gaze like a sponge.

"Sorry. Can't help you there. We're not exactly close." He leaned in and stage-whispered to Tate. "He's not really my type. I'm not into the macho-man thing."

If he was looking for anti-macho, you couldn't get more anti- than Tate.

"I don't suppose you have an address, then?" I asked.

Michael shook his head again. "Sorry."

"Uh, one more thing," I asked, grasping for anything that could help me track down "Mr. Price". "Do you know if Brad's going by his real name or his stage name here?"

Michael squinted, looking off in the distance. "Real name, I think. Dunley?"

I made a mental note of it. At the very least, maybe I could bribe someone in human resources at the Deep Blue to look up his contact info. Of course, that would have to wait until the offices opened again tomorrow morning.

A loud noise sounded over the intercom system, followed by a staticky voice announcing, "Top Hat and Tail number on stage in five."

"That's me," Michael said, gesturing to his bow tie. "Hey, you want to watch the number from the wings?"

Tate clapped his hands and nodded so hard his head was in danger of bobbing loose.

"There's a great spot near the curtains that we reserve for *special* friends," Michael crooned.

Tate squealed with excitement.

At what seemed a stalemate for the night, sleep suddenly sounded so much more fun to me than watching more naked men. "I think I'm actually going to call it a night," I said.

Both pairs of eyes turned to me, almost looking surprised to see I was still there.

"Oh, well, do you want me to walk you back to your room?" Tate asked.

I shook my head. "That's okay. I'm pretty sure I can make it all the way across the street by myself." I blew him a kiss, and he snatched it from the air before letting Michael lead him by the hand to his reserved spot.

Lost in my own thoughts, I barely noticed the cold night air or the milling crowd in the lobby of The Royal Palace. I did, however, pause at my door, the phantom suitcase zipper returning to the forefront of my mind as I entered my room. Glancing carefully around, all seemed as I'd left it. Dresses were still splayed over the couch, my makeup bag emptied across my bathroom sink, and my suitcase still unzipped, contents spilling over the side. I relaxed a bit more as I peeled off my dangerous dress and hung it on the hanger, unstained and none the worse for the wear. After a long, hot shower, I slipped between my sheets, letting thoughts of nearly naked men shove their way into my brain and dance me into exceptionally sweet dreams.

\* \* \*

Banging on my door shot me into a sitting position. I glanced at my curtains for any clue to the time, but I couldn't tell if it was neon or sun glimmering through the cracks. I flopped over and turned my alarm clock toward me. 6am.

"Who in their right mind is up at six?" I grumbled, as I reluctantly pulled the sheets back.

I grabbed a white, fluffy robe with the hotel logo on the pocket and shuffled to the door. I looked through the peephole to find Britton in full workout gear and makeup. Fab.

I opened the door and immediately pointed at the 'Do Not Disturb' placard hanging from the handle. "Does this mean nothing to you?" I huffed.

As though I hadn't said a word, Britton pranced past me and flung herself onto my bed. "I tried to do my work-out this morning, but I just couldn't get my heart into it." She pouted, and I almost felt bad for her.

Almost. It was 6am, after all.

"Coffee?" I ground out, not waiting for an answer before turning to the packets of instant in my tiny kitchenette.

Britton shook her head. "I'm way too jacked up today as it is. You know the police didn't leave until ten last night? Ten!"

"Ouch."

"God, it was awful, Tess," she said, falling back into a spread-eagle position as she complained to the ceiling. "The police dug through positively everything. And I mean *everything*. They even pawed through my tampons. My friggin' tampons!"

I shook my head, pouring a cup of coffee that looked just slightly above the quality of the slushy sludge on the side of the roads this time of year. "That's nuts," I agreed. "I mean, what did they expect to find?"

"I know, right?" she said, her voice going higher and louder. "Like I totally poisoned his drink with killer feminine products. Jerks," she muttered.

"What did Stintner say?" I asked, taking a sip and instantly regretting it. Roadside slush probably would have tasted better. I hated instant.

"He told them to put everything back where they found it and told me to say nothing." She popped up into a sitting position. "You would not believe the questions they asked me. That detective—the one with the pot belly?"

I nodded, even though I hadn't really noticed one plainclothes over another.

"He totally grilled me. Where was I, who had access to the penthouse, did I keep the cupboards locked? Like, stupid stuff, over and over." She paused. "Tess, I have a bad feeling the police think I did something to Dickie."

I had a bad feeling she was right. I sat beside her and put what I hoped was a comforting hand on her back. "I'm sure Stintner will straighten everything out."

"You know I would never, ever hurt Dickie, right Tessie?" she asked me. Her eyes shone with tears and so much sadness, but the Botox fought the good fight everywhere else.

"I know," I told her with 100% conviction. I searched my brain for something to cheer her up, but not actually knowing her very well left me with nothing. Until Mr. Price popped to mind. "Hey, guess who I saw at the male revue last night?"

Instead of cheering her up, her eyebrows turned farther downward. "You went to that gross skin show at the Deep Blue?"

I paused, suddenly feeling as lecherous as the Neanderthal Guy had seemed. "Um, sort of. It was Tate's idea," I mumbled. "Anyway, I figured out who Mr. Price is."

Britton's eyes rounded, and she swatted my arm. "Shut up! How?"

I started to explain to her my arduous process in the security office to view footage, and she stopped me.

"You know, we have state of the art facial recognition software. That would've saved you tons of time."

Even Britton knew about the software? *Damn it, Alfie.*

"Yeah. It would have," I agreed, heavy on the sarcasm. "Anyway, the guy on the tape was one of the dancers in the show last night. Turns out he's also an actor. His name is Brad Dunley."

"Dunley, Dunley," Britton said, churning the name over. "Doesn't ring any bells."

"I was hoping maybe I could coerce someone in HR at the Deep Blue to pull his contact info for me."

Britton's face lit up. Well, the parts that could move did. "Leave it to me, girl. I can get the deets on anyone in this town." She picked up my room phone, dialed a number, and turned away from me, mumbling in hushed tones.

Giving her privacy, I grabbed my pencil skirt and white blouse and went to change in the bathroom. Then I thought better of the blouse after a sniff-test and grabbed a navy T-shirt to pair with my skirt instead. If I tucked it in, and added a long beaded necklace made by one of my artists, it almost looked professional. I made a mental note to do some shopping soon. I had scarcely packed for two days, let alone ten.

When I returned, Britton was just hanging up the phone. "Give me five minutes to change," she bubbled. "I got Brad's address!"

I gaped at her, unable to hide how impressed I was.

She grinned. "Hey, you don't get to be *Mrs*. King and not know a few people who owe you favors." She shot me a wink, before tossing over her shoulder, "You coming?"

Ten minutes later Britton was dressed in a pair of white skinny jeans, a neon green silk top, and a huge white fur coat that looked like a polar bear giving her a hug from behind, and we were in a cab heading down Pioneer Trail, toward the residential section of town.

As we moved away from the resorts, the casinos and souvenir shops gave way to smaller cabins and apartment buildings. Some were trimmed in quaint gingerbread cutouts and log cabin detailing, while others had clearly seen more than their fair share of snowy winters and blistering sunshine—paint peeling, roofs sagging, front yards reduced to large puddles of mud, slush, and fallen pine needles. Dunley's address turned out to be the well-worn variety, a two-story apartment complex with three units upstairs and three down. Layers of paint had been added to the wooden siding in a robin's egg blue, a creamy bone, and a forest green—all of which were showing in various different sections of the building. A set of metal stairs with a sagging railing sat at one end of the building, and two cars minus their tires took up the bulk of the slush covered front yard.

The cab driver pulled in front of the house and then turned to give us the once over. "You want me to wait for you, Mrs. King?" he asked.

"That'd be great, Jack." Britton patted his arm before getting out. I bobbed my head in agreement and followed her.

One day, long ago, someone had cared enough to put in landscaping, as evidenced by the worn, overgrown rock garden surrounding a set of parking slots to the right of the building. I noticed the one with Brad's apartment number painted on the asphalt was empty. I tried not to take that as a bad sign. Maybe he traveled by bus?

As we made our way up the creaking staircase, I was infinitely glad that Britton weighed about as much as a second grader, as the structure groaned under our weight. Brad's apartment was the last one on the far side. Faded green curtains hung in the front window beside a matching wooden door with a plastic number "6" hanging slightly askew. Britton lifted a hand and rapped sharply on it. To our surprised, it creaked open.

I shot a look at Britton and could see my wariness reflected in her gaze back. Who in their right mind left their door open in this neighborhood?

I took a pensive step over the threshold, feeling Britton close behind me.

"Hello?" I called out. "Mr. Dunley?"

The tiny living room was empty except for a few half-empty beer bottles and folding chairs. A darker spot against the faded paint on the wall over an outlet hinted that a fairly large television had hung there at one time not long ago. A small kitchen area sat to our right, littered with pizza boxes, emanating a rotting smell.

"Obviously, Dunley can't afford a cleaning service," Britton observed, waving a hand in front of her scrunched nose.

I agreed, nodding as I pushed open a door off the living room. "Brad? Hello? Anyone here?" A mattress lay on the floor, and a small dresser was pushed up against one wall. All the drawers hung open, empty.

"I don't think he's here," Britton said, coming into the room behind me.

I shoved open the bi-fold closet door to my left. "I don't think his stuff is either," I told her, looking up at a handful of empty wire hangers. No car, no TV, no clothes.

Which meant that, once again, our mysterious Mr. Price was in the wind.

# CHAPTER THIRTEEN

---

Britton stared at me over her coffee cup, faded gray streaks circling her eyes. After hitting a brick wall with Mr. Price-slash-Brad Dunley, I'd insisted we needed caffeine, and lots of it, before figuring out our next move. So we'd taken the cab back to the Royal Palace and were drowning our failures in mocha lattes at the Java Joust.

Yet another of my father's quirky name concoctions.

Emblazoned on the wall that corralled the waiting line was a large coffee bean with a crown. King Bean was in full knight gear, atop his trusty steed with lance in hand. At the other end of the wall, proudly stood another bean in knight gear, sporting a logo way too close to the local big chain competitor. Across the top it read, "Only one coffee meets the royal standard. Our beans rule!"

Ugh, so many lawsuits just waiting to happen right there.

A familiar, shrill voice caused me to glance up at the register.

"Just add it to Alfonso Malone's tab!" Mrs. Ditmeyer bellowed.

The pimple-faced teen behind the counter tried valiantly to calm the woman, but she'd have none of it.

"Unless you would like to wear this hot beverage, I'm leaving, and I'm *not* paying a penny."

Darting to the counter, I placed my hand on the frustrated youth's arm. "Put it on my tab."

Releasing a huge breath, the boy whispered, "Thank you."

Turning what I hoped wasn't a completely forced smile toward the woman, I cooed, "How are you doing this morning, Mrs. Ditmeyer?"

Huffing, she snatched up her supersized latte and narrowed her assessing gaze at me. "I'll be wonderful just as soon as you hire some competent staff." She paused, doing a quick up and down glance of my T-shirt masquerading as professional wear. Like the leopard print muumuu she was wearing was better. After rolling her eyes, she muttered, "Not that I'm holding my breath. Speaking of things I don't really expect to happen, how is the search for my necklace going?"

"Security is working on it," I hedged.

"Right," she huffed, clearly not believing that any more than I did. "Well, while you're working on that, my lawyer is working on a lawsuit."

"Mrs. Ditmeyer, I assure you that in the *unlikely* event the necklace is not recoverable, you will be fully compensated for the value of the item," I told her, recalling that Alfie had said Stintner already filed the paperwork with the insurance company. I vaguely wondered how long it would take them to approve our claim and send a check. And if I was going to be saddled with the cheery Mrs. Ditmeyer until then.

"Money isn't everything," she told me, waggling a chubby finger my way. "That was a family heirloom."

"I understand," I said, channeling my best feather-smoothing voice. "Listen, you didn't happen to encounter anyone named Price while you were staying here, did you?" I asked, going out on a limb.

She scrunched up her brow. "Price?"

"Yes. Young guy, dark hair. Perhaps at the poker tables?"

She waved a hand toward me. "Poker is my husband's game. I don't play."

I pursed my lips, struggling for a connection. "Did you possibly visit your husband at the tables? While you were wearing the necklace?"

She scoffed and gave me a dirty look. "My dear, contrary to what you might think, I don't go flaunting my wealth in public. The only time I even wore the necklace was when we arrived. Then I promptly tucked it away in my safe the minute we set foot in our room. The next time it saw the light of day, I foolishly handed it away to you."

"Right," I mumbled, feeling the accusation in her tone.

She paused and pursed her ruby stained mouth, lipstick feathering out into a coarse lady-stache. "I heard the news report, you know. Someone who's a suspect in her own father's murder shouldn't be running a casino."

I opened my mouth to protest, but before I had the chance she jabbed her free fist onto her hip and jutted her chin in the air, jowls waggling in protest. "I bid you a good day." With one last disapproving scan, she spun around, coffee sloshing from her cup with each stomp toward the elevator.

Britton came up behind me. "They think you killed Dickie, too?"

I turned toward her, not aware how much of the exchange she'd heard. "I don't know," I shrugged. "The media thinks I did." I paused thinking about Agent Ryder. "I don't know what the authorities think." And that was the truth.

Britton pulled me in for a hug. "Then we're in this together, Tess. You and me."

While I would have been hard pressed to find anything Britton and I had in common, the idea that we were "in this" together—whatever mess "this" turned out to be—was oddly comforting. I found myself actually hugging her back.

"Okay, so what did Ditmeyer say about Price?" she asked, finally pulling away and heading back to our table.

"Just that she didn't know him," I said, following her. "She only wore the necklace once. When she arrived at the hotel."

"Well, whoever took it had to have known she had it. So they must have seen her then."

I nodded. "Unfortunately, that doesn't narrow it down a lot."

"Well, let's walk through it," Britton said, sipping at her coffee. "We know whoever Dunley was working with had to be someone with access. An employee, right?"

I nodded. "Right."

"Ditmeyer would have encountered the front desk staff checking in."

I shook my head. "There's no way Tate would be involved in this. I can vouch for him."

Britton nodded. "Agreed. But maybe someone else checked her in? Oh, and what about the bell hop? I'm sure someone took her things to her room for her."

I nodded. "Okay, that's two possibilities."

"And there's room service. I know Mr. Ditmeyer likes a Rueben and a scotch when he first arrives."

"Okay, we're at three staff who could have seen the necklace."

"And there's the parking valet," Britton said, ticking off a third on her fingers.

I perked up in my seat. "The one with the freckles!"

Britton bit her lip. "Freckles, freckles...I don't remember a freckled guy. He must be new."

But my mental hamster was running so fast on her wheel that I hardly heard Britton.

"How about this," I said, a theory coming to me even as I talked it out. "Mrs. Ditmeyer arrives wearing her necklace; the valet sees it when he takes her car. Then he reports back to Mr. Price about the necklace."

Britton puckered her lips. "I don't know. You really think the male stripper is our master safe cracker?"

I bit the inside of my cheek. "You're right. If he's got mad safe cracking skills, what's he doing living in that crap apartment?"

"Okay," Britton said, picking up the scenario where I left off. "So the valet scopes out our whales as they arrive. Dunley pretends to be the high-rolling Mr. Price in order to find out exactly where the whales will be keeping their big ticket items."

"Or, in the case of Ditmeyer's necklace, such knowledge just falls into their laps," I added, wondering how many people might have seen me with that velvet covered box in my hot little hands on its way to the hotel safe. If either Price or the valet had seen me coming from Ditmeyer's room, it wouldn't have taken a rocket scientist to guess what was in the box.

"Right," Britton agreed. "So then who is actually stealing the stuff?"

It hit me like a ton of bricks. "Joe Pesci!" I blurted.

"The actor?" She looked at me like I was nuts.

"No. Well, I'm pretty sure it's not *the* Joe Pesci. A look-alike was at the bar with the valet..." I trailed off, that hamster stating to sprint. "...with Weston!"

At the mention of the man, Britton's eyes narrowed. "That snake? What was he doing here?"

I quickly filled her in on the exchange I'd witnessed, the whole thing taking on new meaning now.

"I'll bet anything that wasn't a tip he was giving the valet. It was a pay-off."

"But why would Weston steal from our guests?" Britton asked, shaking her head. "I mean, he's a royal asshat, but it's not like he needs the money."

"Maybe it isn't about money, I mused. "Look, when Carvell's safe was broken into, what did he do?"

I saw the light bulb go on in Britton's eyes even before she spoke. "He moved over to the Deep Blue."

I nodded. "And someone spread the rumor to Ditmeyer that the hotel was unsafe. Maybe he's not doing it for the money. Maybe he's trying to ruin the Royal Palace's reputation among our whales."

"That sonofa—" Britton trailed off into a litany of swear words, employing the most creative use of the English language I'd heard in a long time. "If he's responsible, I will make him pay," she finally finished. "The man deserves to rot in jail. He's a complete letch. All hands, you know? When I was a beverage attendant..."

"A what?" I interrupted.

"Drink server, cocktail waitress, whatever you want to call it. Dickie always said those names were demeaning, and we deserved a professional title. Anyway, when I was *slinging drinks...*" She paused, brows arched as high as her taut face would allow. With an acknowledging nod from me, she continued, "Weston *always* had to smack my butt when I walked by. Of course, after we got married, Dickie threatened to break both of his hands, and that was the end of that." She smirked, lifting her chin in a proud gesture.

I found myself kind of glad my dad had rescued her from that sort of stuff. Maybe he was the White Knight in some way.

"Well, all we have is theories at the moment," I reminded Britton.

She slurped the last of her latte. "Fine. Then let's go get some evidence. I want to talk to that valet."

That made two of us.

We tossed our paper cups in the trash, and I followed Britton toward the set of glass doors at the front of the casino. Two men in red valet vests milled around the desk in the vestibule, chatting about the latest snowboarding equipment.

"Excuse me," Britton interrupted.

They both snapped to attention. "Mrs. King, what can we help you with?" a short guy with muddy green eyes asked. I watched as he brushed his long hair from his face and straightened his tie.

"Hey, Buckie," she said, addressing him by name. "We're looking for one of the other parking attendants," she told them, then turned to me for the description.

"Tall, dark hair, lots of freckles?"

"Johnny," the taller guy said. "Yeah, he's not here."

"Where is he?" Britton asked.

"I dunno," the first guy told her. "He, uh, didn't show up for work today. Not a real big surprise, though," he added, glancing at his partner.

"Why is that?" I pressed.

"Well, he was sort of lazy. Only liked to take the high rollers. If he didn't smell a big tip, he didn't want to bother. My guess, he won't be back."

I had a bad feeling he was right.

"Is there something I can do for you, ma'am?" the guy asked.

But Britton shook her head. "No, thank you." She paused, then asked. "Did you happen to catch Johnny's last name?"

"Smith," The taller guy said.

"Great, John Smith," I mumbled as we walked back into the lobby. "What do you want to bet that's not his real name?"

"About as much as I want to bet the contact info he gave on his employment application is fake," Britton said, her mind taking the same path mine was.

"So now what?" I asked, my eyes scanning the rows of dinging slots and afternoon regulars at the tables as if the carefully choreographed chaos of the gaming floor might hold the answers.

"Okay, so here's a thought," Britton said, turning to me. "Yesterday, Dickie's death was ruled a homicide. The casino is swarming with media and cops. Today, both our fake Mr. Price and the shady valet are gone. You think maybe the thefts are related to Dickie's murder?"

I blinked at her. Actually, I hadn't. I'd been doing everything I could to push my dad's death and who might have been behind it as far from my thoughts as possible. But now that she'd voiced it, I had to admit, she had a point. "I think it's too much of a coincidence not to be." I paused. "So what does that mean? The valet killed my dad? Mr. Price? Weston?"

Britton cocked her head to the side, sympathy clear in her eyes. "You hate talking about this, don't you?"

What I hated was that I was that transparent. I cleared my throat, putting on my big girl panties. "No. I'm fine. Really," I said, forcing down a lump that had inexplicably lodged itself in my throat.

"Look, I hate it too. Dickie was a good man, and he didn't deserve this. But let's find the bastard who did it. Then you and I can sit with a bottle of Chardonnay and have a good long cry about it."

A laugh escaped me, and before I could stop myself I was nodding in agreement. "Deal."

"And to answer your question," Britton said, "my money is on Weston. He had the most to lose if Dickie found out he was behind the thefts."

"You think my dad figured it out?"

Britton shrugged. "He was crazy smart. It's totally possible. Maybe he even confronted Weston about it, threatened to go to the authorities."

"But how would Weston get into the penthouse to poison the DynoDrink?"

Britton opened her mouth to speak, then quickly shut it with a click. "Oh. Good point." She paused. "You think he hired someone to do his dirty work? Like the valet?"

But before I could follow that train of thought any further, my phone buzzed in my pocket. I pulled it out and saw Rafe's face on the display, unable to help the grin that hit my cheeks as I answered.

"Hello?"

"Hey, beautiful," he said.

I felt warmth instantly flood my face—and other parts of my body—at the sentiment. "Hey, yourself," I managed to reply. I saw Britton raise a questioning eyebrow my way. I ducked my head, trying to disguise the blush I could feel quickly spreading.

"How are you holding up?" he asked. "Alfie chase the reporters out of your way?"

I nodded. "He did. Thanks, Rafe."

Britton's eyes widened, and she whispered, "Oh, that's who has you blushing like a nun in a sex-shop."

I attempted to put my finger to her lips to shush her, and turned away, forcing my voice to a casual tone. "What's up?"

"You and me, dinner tonight. You free?"

I felt my heart beat double time. Was he asking me out? On a *date*? "Dinner tonight?" I repeated. Teen-me busied herself doing cartwheels of glee while I worked on getting my heart rate under control. "Uh, yeah. Sounds great."

"Excellent! I have a wicked idea for a snowboarding event to bring in more casino guests. You know, maybe offer free lift tickets to everyone who books a room."

I paused, heart instantly slowing. Not a date. A business meeting. I closed my eyes and cursed Teen-me for celebrating prematurely. Of course it wasn't a date. Rafe dated size-two, pink-fluff-wearing Barbie managers. He didn't date failed artists turned gallery curators. And he certainly didn't date his temporary boss turned snowboarding pal who was going to clear out of town just as soon as she possibly could.

Not, mind you, that I wanted to date him either. The flush in my cheeks was probably just the hotel's heat turned up too high.

I realized he'd been talking, and tried to tune in before I missed the entire conversation.

"...anyway, I think it could be really good to get some positive publicity surrounding the casino right now, you know?"

"Absolutely!" I said, forcing the cheerfulness maybe just a little too hard. "Should I meet you somewhere?"

"Nah, I'll pick you up at your room. About seven-thirty? I heard about the knockout dress you wore last night. Feel free to wear that again," he hinted before he hung up.

*Down Teen-me.*

I was just telling myself that Rafe's nature was the flirtatious charmer whether he meant to flirt or not, when I looked up and spotted his polar opposite walking toward me.

Agent Ryder.

If Rafe was naturally flirtatious, Ryder was naturally guarded. I wasn't sure which was more frustrating.

"Ms. King. Mrs. King," he said, nodding at each of us respectively.

"Agent Ryder," I said, trying to match the detached professionalism in his voice even though the way he looked me up and down in my T-shirt and pencil skirt was a keen reminder I'd been wearing a whole lot less the last time he'd seen me.

"You're that Fed, right?" Britton said, breaking through the awkward in the air.

Ryder turned his attention to her. "I am with the FBI," he confirmed.

"Good. Because we know who killed Dickie."

Ryder raised one eyebrow ever so slightly. "You do?"

Britton nodded emphatically. Then she nudged me in the ribs with her elbow. "Tell him, Tessie."

"Me?" I squeaked out.

Ryder's quizzical gaze shifted my way.

I cleared my throat. "Right. Okay. Sure." Then I proceeded to tell him our theory about the valet, Dunley, and Joe Pesci's crime ring headed by Weston, half waiting for him to tell me I'd been watching as many crime dramas as Britton. But at this point, I was willing to risk looking a little nuts if it cleared the name of my dad's legacy. "Look, if my dad found out, it would give them ample motive to want to get rid of him," I finished.

"Our money's on Weston," Britton added. "He's a royal asshat."

I could have sworn I saw the corner of Ryder's mouth twitch upward ever so slightly. "That's an interesting theory."

I perked up. Maybe he would take us seriously after all.

"But it's just that," he added. "A theory."

The perk deflated instantly. "Hey, evidence is your job," I pointed out. "Which should be easy enough to get. Just go talk to Weston."

Ryder narrowed his eyes at me and crossed his arms over his chest. "And say what? That we would like to talk to him about a dancer at his club, a vanishing valet, and some guy who looks like Joe Pesci?"

I bit my lip. Well, put like that I did sound nuts.

"Ask him where he was the morning Dickie died," Britton suggested.

"We have."

I blinked. "You have?"

More eye narrowing. "I am a professional investigator, Ms. King. Of course we asked. He's a known rival of your father's. He was one of our first suspects."

I suddenly felt not only nuts but about two feet tall. "He was?"

Ryder nodded slowly.

"And I'm guessing he's not now?"

Ryder shook his head just as slowly.

"Why the heck not?" Britton yelled. "The man's a snake."

"That may be, but he's got an alibi. Weston was seen at the Deep Blue by over a hundred employees who can account for his whereabouts all day long. Not to mention security footage backing up their story."

I looked up at the ever-present black cameras above us. Of course there would be footage.

"Then he hired someone," Britton spouted, throwing her hands in the air. "The valet. Or even Joe Pesci! God, can't you people see how obvious it is? That's it, I'm getting Alfie on this," she said, pulling out her cell and dialing.

There went that tick at the corner of Ryder's mouth again. I could swear it was even threatening to turn into a full-fledged grin as Britton stomped toward the elevator, stabbing the up button.

He turned to me. "Is she always like that?"

I jutted my chin out, suddenly feeling defensive on her behalf. "Passionate? Pro-active? Determined? Yes."

"Boy, you two make quite a pair."

I wasn't sure if that was a compliment or a jab. But I didn't have a chance to analyze it further as his grin disappeared as quickly as it had arrived, and he was all business again. "Look, leave the investigating to the authorities, okay? We know what we're doing. We will bring your father's killer to justice."

"Meaning you don't believe me at all," I translated.

"I didn't say that," he hedged. "But I can't just haul someone like Weston in for questioning based on a hunch."

"Even a good hunch?"

"Even a good hunch," he said definitively.

I pursed my lips, staring him down. He did his patented poker face. Finally I cracked first.

"So what are you doing here anyway?"

He took a deep breath, letting it out slowly through his nose. "There's been a development in the case. And I..." He paused, the stony face slipping just the slightest bit into something softer, almost emotional. "...I wanted you to hear it from me first. Before the media."

Uh oh. Emotion from Agent Poker Face was not good. I licked my lips, steeling myself for whatever came next. "What is it?"

Ryder took a step forward, his voice lowering. "We found the poison that killed your dad."

"Where?" I asked, already fearing the answer.

"The penthouse. I'm sorry, Tessie," he said, putting a hand on my arm. "It belongs to Britton."

# CHAPTER FOURTEEN

———

"No, way," I said, shaking my head violently against Ryder's suggestion. "Britton did not kill my father."

"I know it's hard to think badly of family—"

"She's not my family," I shot out, more from instinct than anything else.

"Okay," he said. "But she is a suspect."

"Seriously?" I pointed to Britton, waiting on the elevator, dressed in her powder pink tights, and matching baby-doll T with Hello Kitty on the front, twisting a blonde lock of hair around her finger as she talked into her phone. "Does she look like a criminal mastermind to you?"

"Looks can be deceiving," he said. "And I have to point out that she doesn't exactly look like a grieving widow, either."

"People grieve in different ways."

"Tessie, a massive amount of hydromorphone was found in your father's system."

"And this points to Britton how?" I challenged.

"A bottle of Dilaudid, which is the prescribed oral form of hydromorphone, was found in Britton's medicine cabinet. Hers were the only prints on the bottle."

"Maybe the killer wiped it clean," I suggested.

Ryder raised an eyebrow my way. "At which point we would have found *no* prints."

"Unless Britton touched it *after* the killer," I said, proud to put my hours of *CSI* watching to use.

Ryder rubbed the bridge of his nose between his thumb and forefinger. "Which, again, is a nice *theory*."

"Hey, pal, all you have is theories, too," I pointed out.

"Did Britton tell you where she was when your father's drink was spiked?" Ryder asked, ignoring my statement.

I opened my mouth to respond, but then shut it with a click when I realized that, in fact, she hadn't. I guess I'd assumed she was at Pilates or getting her nails done or somewhere like that. But I hadn't actually asked her.

"No," I admitted. "But I'm sure the cameras caught her somewhere," I said, gesturing up to the black circles above us.

Only Ryder's stony expression made that "surety" waiver on the spot.

"Actually, they don't," he told me.

I bit my lip. "Maybe she was in the penthouse?"

There went that eyebrow heading north again. "Exactly my point." Ryder punctuated it with a nod my way.

I shook my head. "The penthouse is big. Someone could have spiked the drink without her even knowing. She could have been in the shower, in the den, or sleeping off a late night martini binge in the bedroom." But even as I defended her, my mind was reeling. Why hadn't Britton told me she didn't have an alibi?

"Look, I'll admit the police don't yet have enough to issue a warrant for Britton," Ryder told me. "But I know you two are close, so I just wanted you to know. And to...be careful," he ended, that softer look returning to his features.

I bit my lip, nodding even as a million thoughts swirled through my head. I *thought* Britton and I were getting close. But the truth was, I'd only really spent any time with her these last few days. What did I really know about Britton anyway? That she was a former cocktail waitress who clearly did *not* want to go back to that life. Had things been as rosy as she painted between her and my dad? Or had they actually been having problems?

"You okay?" Ryder asked, putting a hand on my arm.

I nodded again, unable to form a coherent thought, let alone voice one.

"Look, just lay low for awhile, Tessie. Leave the investigating to the authorities. Take some time to de-stress, maybe go to the spa."

Why was it every guy thought I needed a spa day?

But instead of arguing I just nodded dumbly again. "Yeah. Sure."

He smiled, patted my arm, and walked off toward the main entrance, presumably heading to gather more evidence with his police pals to gain that warrant.

I watched, my mind racing at full tilt. I knew for a fact that Britton was not as dumb as she looked. Had she been playing me all along? What if she and my dad had been having problems? What if she'd been the one who'd killed him, then wanted to play investigator with me just to divert my attention from her? It had worked. I hadn't even thought to ask Britton where she'd been when he'd died. She'd had means and opportunity to kill him.

I took a deep breath, pulling myself together. It was time to find out if she'd had motive, too.

I waited for Ryder to disappear out the doors and into the sunshine before I made my way to the elevator. I punched the up arrow, then once the carriage arrived, hit the button for the 4th floor. Stintner's offices were at the end of a long corridor that housed the casino's human resources, accounting, and legal departments. I pushed through the glass doors of legal and Stintner's secretary greeted me immediately.

"Ms. King, to what do we owe the pleasure today?" the polished brunette in a sharp blouse and blazer asked.

"I was hoping that Mr. Stintner might have a minute to speak with me," I told her, glancing behind her at the short hallway leading to more inner offices.

"I believe he does. Please have a seat." She waved me over to a couch before disappearing down the hall.

The waiting area was furnished much the same as the rest of the hotel—tasteful, clean, modern. I didn't see any evidence of Stintner hiring his own decorator, though a couple photos of the lake graced the walls, the stunning blue a contrast to the pale beige wallpaper. Along one side of the room ran the same tall windows as in the penthouse, the view of the white-capped mountains here almost as stunning. I drank them in, hoping the calming scene would wear off on me.

"Tessie."

Stintner's voice startled me, pulling me away from the serene landscape.

"Mr. Stintner. I'm glad you could see me," I told him, regaining my composure.

"Of course. Please, come on back." He motioned toward his office with one hand and smoothed his silver comb-over with the other.

I followed him down the hall and into his corner office with yet another prime view of the mountains. A dark, cherry wood desk took up the bulk of the room, with matching bookcases and a small liquor cabinet filling the far wall. A pair of leather club chairs sat in front of the bookcase, a small table holding a decorative globe between them.

Stintner sank into a black, leather chair behind the desk. "I hope everything is okay."

I sat in one of the club chairs, hearing the leather squeak beneath me. "I do, too," I told him, honestly. "Look, I...I'm not sure how to ask this," I said, trying to remember just what sort of stuff came under client-attorney privilege. But, considering my father was dead, he couldn't really complain, right?

"What is it?" Stintner asked, his bushy brows falling in concern.

"I'd like to see my dad's will," I blurted out.

His eyebrows didn't relax any. "I believe we already went over the terms for your inheritance."

I nodded. "We did. But I'd really like to know how his other assets were split."

"I see," he said, his gaze slowly assessing me. "Well, I suppose you have a right to that information. But there's really not a whole lot else to know." He shuffled through his desk drawer and pulled out a thick folder, perching his glasses on the end of his nose. "Is there anything in particular you're looking for?"

I nodded, feeling knots form in my stomach. "What did he leave Britton?"

Stintner paused, peering at me over the glasses. But if he was curious why I wanted to know, he didn't say so. "Your father had most everything staked in this casino. Even his shares are leveraged for loans to keep it afloat. There wasn't much to leave."

I narrowed me eyes. "Define not much."

Stintner sighed. "It's more complicated than that. She has a non-controlling number of shares, some stakes in a couple of funds he invested in, but very little else. Your father was quite short on liquid assets."

"So, what are you saying?" I asked. "That my dad was broke?"

"I'm saying, Mrs. King will have to make some lifestyle changes in the near future," he answered. "The shares are worthless unless she cashes out, and even then she'll get pennies on the dollar with the way Mr. King had them leveraged. The cars, the furnishings, all of that belongs to the casino. There were a couple of personal bank accounts, of course," he said, shifting through the papers again. "But the balances on all of these combined is not significant. In all honesty, Britton will be lucky to get a decent studio apartment with it."

"Apartment? What about the penthouse?"

Stintner removed his reading glasses and folded them on the stack of papers. "The penthouse will belong to whoever is named chairman after you leave. Britton has less than a month to vacate the property, according to the lease agreement with the casino board of directors."

My mind tripped over the memory of all the boxes Britton had been packing, how sparse the place had looked. She wasn't just packing up my dad's things; she was packing up the entire place. Despite my previous suspicion of her, I felt a pang of remorse.

"You're sure that's all?" I asked, peering over the desk at the paperwork.

Stintner nodded. "Quite sure. I'm sorry, Tessie, but if you're looking for money, there just wasn't any."

I shook my head. "No, I was just..." I trailed off, loath to admit that I'd just been looking for a motive for Britton to have killed my dad. "Never mind. It's not important now," I finished, standing and backing out of his office. "Thank you for your time."

I made my way to the elevator and hit the button for the penthouse. The front doors stood open, the moving crew obviously in the midst of removing items from the place. As I walked into the penthouse, the knots tightened in my gut. More boxes were stacked around the perimeter of the living room, bookcases and curio cabinets left bare. Though, I could plainly see that the more expensive items were staying—the crystal chandeliers, the leather sofas, the Persian rugs and the Vermeer. I felt a weight in my chest at the thought that someone new would soon be occupying my dad's "castle".

"Tess, is that you?" Britton called from down the hall.

I cleared the emotion out of my throat. "Yeah."

"Be out in a sec," she called. Then true to her word, a moment later she appeared, dressed in a pair of teeny running shorts, hot pink spandex top, and pristine white running shoes. With pink laces. "Hey," she said. "I've got to go work out some aggression in the gym. Ugh, that Alfie is such a chauvinist, you know?"

I nodded. But chatting about Alfie's backwards views on feminism wasn't why I was here. "Why didn't you tell me you were leaving?" I asked.

Britton blinked at me. "Leaving?"

"The penthouse. The casino," I said, gesturing to the stacks of boxes.

"Oh." Her face fell as far as the Botox would allow. "Right. Well, I guess I just figured you knew. I mean, I figured Stintner read you the will."

I shook my head. "No, he didn't. At least, not until today. I...I had no idea my dad didn't leave you anything. Britton, I'm so sorry."

Britton shrugged. "It's just stuff," she said, though I could see the words didn't quite make it to her eyes, now threatening to brim with shining tears. "None of it really matters, you know. I mean, I know Dickie left me what he could. It wasn't like he was planning on checking out, you know?"

"I'm so sorry, Britton," I said again. And I was. Not just that circumstances had left her high and dry but that I'd ever suspected her of hurting my dad over money. I could clearly tell that Britton liked her lifestyle here—and who wouldn't? But the tears in her eyes now were not over the end of her stint as the reigning Mrs. King, but over her lost king. "Can I do anything to help?" I asked.

Britton let out a big breath and walked to the large patio doors, leaning against the fogging glass. She wrapped her arms across herself, hugging her shoulders. "I just want to wake up in the morning with Dickie by my side. I want him to wrap me up in a hug so tightly I can't breathe and have him joke about how love hurts sometimes." She paused and drew a heart on the misty glass, adding her initials and my father's to the center. "I knew I wouldn't get much of anything in the will. But, that's not what Dickie and I were about. I am kind of bummed to have to move from here. This was the only place that ever felt like home to me, you know?" She looked over her shoulder at me, tears still welling in her eyes. "But I wouldn't have felt right taking anything, even if he had left me a pile of cash. I came into the relationship with nothing."

"And now you have nothing again," I murmured, channeling her melancholy.

Britton shook her head so adamantly her ponytail came loose as she turned back toward me, tears now freely flowing down her cheeks. "No. I had five of the best years of my life, filled with more love than I ever imagined possible. I'll keep that with me always. That's *totally* not nothing." She released a heavy sigh.

I stared at my father's wife, really seeing her for the first time. I'd seen Britton before, but it was as the gold digger I thought she was, the harlot-slash-prostitute my mother thought she was, or the airhead most people saw her as. She was none of those. I'd been looking at her through the eyes of a spoiled teenager who didn't get things exactly the way she wanted or the stilted view of my mother who thought Britton and my father embodied the end of the world. I wasted so many years complaining that things hadn't gone my way, instead of embracing the way they were. Now, it was too late.

The tears flowing down my face surprised both of us.

"Oh, honey," she muttered as she pulled me into her arms.

"I'm so sorry," I whispered, "for so very many things."

We spent a good five minutes sniffling and sobbing before she gently pushed me away, wiping at her cheeks.

"Wow, that was therapeutic," she said, attempting a smile.

I couldn't help grinning. "So, you said you talked to Alfie?" I asked, focusing on a less emotional subject in order to get my running mascara under control.

Britton nodded, then sniffed loudly. "I did. I told him Weston killed Dickie."

"And what did he say to that?"

She shrugged. "The usual. That the police were looking into it, that we should stay out of it, that I needed—"

"—to go relax at the spa," I finished for her.

She grinned in earnest this time. "How did you know?"

"He's so predictable. Plus, Agent Ryder pretty much told me the same thing."

"Yeah, what was he doing here anyway?" Britton asked.

Not for the first time, I noticed that very little got past her. "Nothing," I mumbled. "He was just...looking into stuff." That was so lame even to my ears, but the last thing I wanted to do was add another layer of worry to Britton's already heavy load. She had lost a spouse, she was being kicked out of her home and facing a huge question mark about her future now that the Royal Palace fund had dried up for her. Besides, I had complete confidence that the police would soon realize Britton had not killed my dad.

Okay, I had 75% confidence.

"Anyway, I'm gonna hit the gym," Britton said. "A good long run on the treadmill is what I need to clear my head, you know?"

I nodded, though I thought a good long nap might be more my speed.

We parted ways as the elevator let me off at the 5th floor for my room and Britton continued down to the lower level gym. My brain was still lost in thought over everything that I'd learned that day as I made my way down the hall and opened the door to my room.

Then froze.

The cushions of my loveseat were tossed beside the bed, which was stripped down to the mattress, sheets, comforter, and pillows strewn across the floor. My clothes were draped everywhere with my suitcase turned upside down in the bottom of the closet. Cosmetics, personal items, and hotel knickknacks were strewn across the floor in every direction. The scene looked a whole lot like Britton's penthouse when the cops had been searching it.

My breath caught in my throat. Someone had ransacked my room.

I quickly pulled out my cell from my pockets, fingers hovering over the keyboard to dial Alfie, when a sound behind me pulled my attention.

I spun to see what it was. But I never got the chance, as pain exploded on the side of my head, the ground rushed up to meet me, and the phone flew from my hand.

Just before everything went black.

# CHAPTER FIFTEEN

———

Thanks to my mother's constant lectures on the evils of all things casino, Tahoe, or gambling related, I had never been a huge drinker. Though when I was faced with being a bridesmaid for the third time in one summer after all three of my best friends from college had found their Mr. Rights, and I'd found a stray cat, I will admit to overindulging just a bit at the open bar at the reception. Especially after one of the groomsmen had mistaken me for my BFF's *older* aunt. Several rounds with Jose Cuervo and one night spent drooling on my BFF's couch later, I'd awoken with a headache that had extended all the way from my scalp down to my toes, the pounding so intense I'd sworn my brain was seconds from actually leaking out of my ears.

This was worse.

I blinked, instantly regretting the decision as pain numbed my senses, my head pounding with the violence of a thousand drum lines.

"Tess," I heard a voice calling, though it sounded far away. And under water.

I struggled through the fog enveloping my brain to place it.

"Tessie?" the voice called again. Deep, smooth, worried.

I forced myself to blink again, which was slightly less painful this time, slowly letting the world come into focus. A figure in front of me emerged from the fog, his dark eyebrows drawn in concern over the greenest pair of eyes on the planet.

"There you are," Rafe said, his fingers sliding across my cheek, his other arm cinching me against him. "You had me worried, hon."

I did some more blinking before deciding to try speech. "What happened?" I croaked out.

Rafe shook his head. "You tell me. I came to pick you up for dinner and found the door open and you on the floor." He drew in a shaky breath. "Your place looks like hell."

I focused past him to the chaos of my belongings scattered in every direction, the scene I'd first witnessed slowly flooding back to me.

"Someone hit me," I said.

Rafe pursed his lips together. "Who?" he asked, looking like he was ready to clobber the offender.

"I wish I knew. He hit me from behind."

"You didn't see anything?" he asked.

I bit my lip. "No. I heard something though," I said, memories flooding.

"Something like a..."

"I don't know," I admitted. I tried to sit up to assess the damage to my stuff. Bad idea. The room started to spin, and I instantly fell back on my elbows.

"Whoa, careful," Rafe said. "Paramedics are on the way."

"No, I don't need..." But the sharp pain on the side of my head cut my words short.

"Humor me and let them at least look you over," he said.

As if on cue, a knock sounded at the door, and a voice yelled, "Paramedics."

Rafe left my side for the split second it took to open the door for them before returning right back to me. Two men and a mobile gurney pushed through the door.

"Did you move her?" the bigger guy barked at Rafe.

He shook his head. "She tried to sit up."

"That's not good if she has any kind of spinal injury," he huffed. "Hold her still."

Rafe's arms froze around me.

"I'm awake." I raised my hand, waving at the men.

As though I'd not spoken a word, the two men broke into their routine, shining lights in my eyes, taking vitals, and blurting what sounded like gibberish back and forth.

"There doesn't seem to be a concussion, but we're going to need to take her in for tests," the lead medic said as he ripped the Velcro open on a neck brace.

"I'm awake, and I'm fine," I said again, slapping the paramedic's hands away. I forced myself past the wild drumming in my head and into a sitting position.

He stood tall in front of me, blue gloved hands gripping his hips. "Well, ma'am, we can't force you to go."

"Good, then I'll stay."

The other guy shoved a clipboard in front of me. "If you'll just sign off there, we'll leave you be. Come to the Emergency Room if you have any of the symptoms listed on the sheet."

He turned his glare toward Rafe. "Please make sure she stays awake for at least a couple of hours to watch for any speech problems or eyesight changes."

After scrawling what I was almost positive to be my signature fairly close to the line indicated, the second in command shoved the carbon copy into my hands. They simultaneously cast a wary look over their shoulders as they wheeled the gurney into the hall and disappeared toward the elevator.

Rafe pushed the hair away from my temple and winced right along with me when he touched the knot on the side of my head. "That's a pretty impressive lump. Are you sure you don't want to go to the hospital."

"I'm sure," I grumbled. Something about all of the illnesses and needles all bundled up in one building made me positive.

Rafe pulled out his cell phone and started dialing.

"Now who are you calling?" I asked, peeking at the screen.

"Alfie. He needs to know."

I groaned. "Are you sure?"

"Smart man," Alfie's voice boomed from the doorway. "I was caught up with an issue on the floor, or I'd have been here before the ambulance." He dropped to his knees on the other side of me, grabbed my chin, and whipped my face toward him. The room did a tilt-a-whirl impression. If I had eaten anything recently, it would've made an encore presentation.

I squinted up at him, pushing his hand away. "Do you understand the concept of gentle?"

His thick brows scrunched into one, but a glimmer of a smile danced in his eyes as he looked up toward Rafe. "As long as she keeps being a smart ass, we don't really need to worry."

"She says she was attacked," Rafe said, not sharing his levity. I silently crushed on him all the harder for it.

Alfie's eyes surveyed the room. "Anything missing?" he asked. I was fairly certain he was talking to me though his eyes were on the mess.

"I don't know," I answered honestly. "I haven't had a chance to look through it all yet. But I didn't have a whole lot with me for anyone to take."

Alfie stepped through the room, picking up a pair of shoes, lifting a dress to look underneath. "I've got my guys going through the security footage of the hallway now."

"Be sure to use that facial recognition software," I mumbled.

"What was that?" Alfie asked.

"Nothing." I blinked innocently at him.

"Hmm," he muttered. "Well, I hate to tell you this, Ms. King, but this doesn't look like a robbery. It looks like a warning." Alfie paused to let that sink in before spinning on me. "Who have you gone and pissed off now?"

I narrowed my eyes at him. "I haven't pissed off anyone."

Alfie snorted. "Mrs. Ditmeyer would disagree, but I doubt the old girl has this kind of anger management issue."

"Maybe it was random?" Rafe piped up. "Some kids or something."

As much as I wanted that to be true, I doubted anyone in the room believed it.

"This wasn't random," I said, shooting down that comforting theory. "It was Joe Pesci." I sat up, trying to steady myself, against the room dancing around me.

"Excuse me?" Alfie asked.

"Not *the* Joe Pesci. At least, I don't think it is," I explained.

Alfie looked from me to Rafe. "How hard did she hit her head?" he asked.

I closed my eyes, took a deep breath and did my best to sound convincing as I told them both about what I'd seen in the lounge, the actor, the missing valet, the thefts and Britton's theory about Weston being behind it all.

"Britton mentioned something about Weston earlier," Alfie admitted, almost to himself. I hoped he felt just a little guilty now for not looking into it. "But I highly doubt he'd go around whacking our guests."

"But he might send his henchman to do it," I said. I refrained from pointing out that I was not a *guest* at the Royal Palace, but the *owner.* At least for eight more days.

Alfie drew a long breath in through his nose. "Fine. I'll have Maverick look through the tapes for any sign of 'Joe Pesci.'" He finished off the statement with a pair of air quotes that told me he wasn't totally convinced he was going to find anything at all. "In the meantime," he continued, "it's not safe for you to stay here. I'll send someone to move your things up to the penthouse for the time being."

The stern scowl on his face kept me from arguing. Not that I really wanted to stay in my room after all that had happened. Instead, I nodded meekly.

Alfie's phone rang, and he pushed the button on his earpiece. "Malone," he said before lumbering out into the hall to talk.

"Don't worry," Rafe told me. "Alfie won't let that guy get away with this." While I'm sure it was meant to be reassuring, I couldn't help feeling like every guy in my life was telling me to sit back and let them take care of things. Which was turning out just dandy so far.

"Hey," he added, tucking a few strands of hair behind my ear. "You hungry?"

I knew I should be. But as I glanced around my disheveled room, all I really wanted was to sleep for about three days. Only I didn't feel safe enough anywhere for that to happen. "I guess I need to try to eat something," I finally gave in.

"I'll call down and tell them to hold our table."

I couldn't even imagine trying to fight the hem of the dangerous dress with my head pounding, but my little black funeral dress would be passable with the slacks and v-neck sweater Rafe was wearing. "I'll go change, then."

I pushed against the couch, attempting to use it for leverage, but my knees buckled. Rafe's hands slid around my waist and pulled me to my feet. I looked up into his face as he pulled me against him. Time stood still for one long moment as his stubbled jaw tensed with concern, his amazingly bright green eyes roving my face, his lips so close I could almost taste them.

Then he gently set me down on the sofa. Teen-me whimpered in protest.

"Scratch changing," Rafe said, seemingly oblivious to the moment. "In fact, maybe we should just do room service."

"No!" I said. Maybe a little more forceful than I'd meant to. "No, I mean, let's go somewhere else. I'm...I'm not sure I can stay here." Which was the truth. My cozy little haven suddenly had a menacing taint to it.

As if he instinctually understood, Rafe nodded, made the call to the restaurant, and ten minutes later we were standing in front of the Golden Chalice.

The Chalice was one of the finer dining experiences at the Royal Palace. During the day, most people dined in khakis and sundresses, but when the mountain shadows fell over the casino, the unwritten dress code got a bit ritzier. As we stood in line waiting on the maître de, a woman pranced by in a full length formal dress on the arms of a man in jacket and tie. I suddenly missed the short dress.

Obviously sensing my discomfort, Rafe grabbed my hand and tucked it in the crook of his arm. "You look beautiful."

I glanced up at him and forced a smile to my face. "You're full of crap, but thank you for trying."

"How's your head?"

I ran a light finger over the knot at my temple with my free hand. "I think the bump is getting bigger," I moaned.

"Then I think we're line-jumping," he said, tugging my hand toward the front.

The small framed man dressed in a starched white shirt, black pants and long apron turned an annoyed face our way at the intrusion. That is until recognition animated his features. "Mr. Lorenzo, Ms. King, why has my staff kept you waiting in line?" He waved frenzied arms resembling one of the large inflatables businesses put in their parking lots to drum up customers. "Please, allow our VIPs through."

Rafe slipped the man some money as they shook hands. "I'm so sorry to throw my weight around like that, but Ms. King has a bit of a headache and needs to sit down."

I almost resisted rolling my eyes. His words made me sound like a prima donna trying to get her way.

But they did the trick.

"Oh, you poor thing. Right this way." He waved the menus in his hand toward a table in the center of the room. "The best seat in the house," he assured us.

As we were seated, the window next to us afforded a view of the swimming pool, illuminated with floating candles and ambient lighting. The sun was setting along the horizon, dark orange outlining the jagged mountain tops in the distance. Several fond memories of my father and me sitting at the very same table filtered past the throbbing pain. He'd order a dirty martini and oysters for himself and a Shirley Temple for me before the host even got us settled.

"It's good to see you smile," Rafe said as the waiter stopped at our table. "Well, I was going to order wine for us, but with that nasty bump, we'd better stick to iced tea." He held up two fingers and the waiter disappeared.

He picked up his menu, casually scanning it. "So, what does one eat after being bludgeoned?" His eyes sparkled teasingly over the top of his menu at me.

"I don't know what tradition dictates," I played back at him, "but I'm leaning toward the Chicken Bella."

"Superb choice," the waiter interjected as he walked up to the table. His pen hovered over his order pad until I nodded.

"I'll have the same," Rafe said. Then as the waiter walked away, he added, "You know, I was going to float some ideas for the casino by you tonight, but if you're not up to it..."

I shook my head. "No, no. I'm fine. And, actually, I'd love to hear your ideas." Which was only half true. What I'd have loved was to sit and stare at the sunset, reminiscing about old times. But I knew that thoughts of old times would lead to thoughts of my dad. Which would lead to thoughts of who had killed him, who was stealing from our hotel guests, and who had hit me over the head. All of which were not going to do my headache any good. So, while I'll admit to only half listening, the change of pace was a welcome distraction.

Rafe's spiel was as focused and well thought out as any sales pitch I'd ever heard. He had big ideas about transforming the image of the Palace, making it more family friendly like some of the Vegas casinos. He wanted to create an atmosphere that welcomed the young and old alike to the slopes, not just the throw-back crowd my dad had catered to. While his ideas had merit, I knew they required money. And that was something the casino was sorely lacking at the moment. While he talked, I kept checking my phone for any news from Alfie, but as our plates were placed in front of us, I forced myself to pay closer attention to Rafe.

"I discussed most of this with your father, you know, before..." Rafe's words trailed off as he placed his napkin in his lap, his face contorting with concern.

Pushing around a large, sauce-coated mushroom with my fork, I took a deep breath and let it out slowly. "It's okay to talk about my father's death. I'm coming to terms with it."

He shook his head as he set down his fork and knife, leaning forward and propping his elbows on the table. "I just can't believe someone poisoned him, and in his health shake, no less."

I froze.

I felt my skin tingling, my foggy brain suddenly focused with laser precision on his words.

The news that my father had been murdered was obviously no secret. However, the fact that poison was introduced to his DynoDrink had yet to be disclosed to the general public. I carefully went back over every conversation Rafe and I had in the last few days. I was certain I hadn't mentioned it to him. So how did he know?

I attempted to set my fork carefully on the table. The resounding squeal of the tines scraping against the plate from my shaking hand nearly made my fillings jump from my teeth. I dropped the fork on my napkin, using every ounce of my strength to push past the pounding headache and the urge to grab him by the front of the sweater to interrogate him.

"His health shake?" I asked, playing dumb.

Rafe paused, forkful of food halfway to his mouth. "His what?"

"Health shake," I repeated, my heart racing. "You just said his health shake was poisoned. How would you know that?"

In the silence that followed, my mind ran rampant. Rafe had reportedly been doing publicity on the mountain at the time the drink was poisoned, but he could've easily slipped back to the casino. The staff wouldn't have given him a second look. He was in and out of the penthouse all the time to chat with my dad, according to Britton.

Which begged the question—what did I really even know about Rafe other than the love-struck musings of a teenage crush and how the media portrayed him? He was the one who turned my father on to the health drink. I'm sure he could have easily had access to Britton's medicine cabinet. Maybe he'd floated these same ideas to my father and hadn't been happy with the way he'd responded. Unhappy enough to do something drastic.

And Rafe said he'd found me on the floor this evening, but what if he'd really been the one who'd put me there?

"Rafe?" I prompted when I realized he still hadn't answered. "How do you know about the health shake?"

He broke the silence with a deceptively casual shrug. "Wasn't that how he died?"

I nodded slowly. "But I wasn't aware that was public knowledge."

"I guess I just assumed," he said, covering the statement quickly with a sip from his iced tea.

"You just *assumed* he was poisoned and *assumed* that it was his DynoDrink?" I asked. "That's a lot of great guessing on your part."

Rafe paused. He set his drink down. Then his face broke into his charming bad-boy grin, the one he pulled out for the cameras and groupies. "Okay, you caught me. I've been listening to the hotel rumor mill. Some girls from housekeeping saw the police taking cans of the stuff from the penthouse. I admit it, I'm a gossip. Please don't tell anyone. It will ruin my image." Then he winked, as if letting me in on his private joke.

"The police took a lot of stuff from the penthouse," I said slowly. "What made you so sure that about the DynoDrink?"

Rafe shrugged. "Well, if I were going to poison someone, I'd put it in the DynoDrink." He leaned forward, as if sharing a secret. "I know I'm a sponsor, but have you smelled that stuff?" He waved a hand in front of his nose.

I watched his charming act as I mused that it was an interesting choice of words. *If I were going to poison someone...* It was possible he was telling the truth. I mean, hadn't Britton made the same leap about the health shake? Then again, it was just as possible he was covering.

I tried to look for his tell, anything that said he was lying. The only problem was that all my father had taught me about catching liars and cheaters was lost to my inability to filter past my own feelings. This was way too personal. I wanted to believe Rafe. Which meant it was possible I was missing something. Then there was the steady drum beat in my head which didn't help things.

My phone jingled to life in my purse. I pulled it out, thankful for respite, and saw Alfie's face gracing the screen. I swiped the phone on. "Tessie."

"We found your Joe Pesci look-alike," Alfie growled in my ear, almost sounding unhappy to admit that such a guy actually existed.

For the first time that night, I felt my spirits rise. "You did? Where?"

Alfie's voice held zero hint of humor as he answered. "He's swimming with the fishes."

# CHAPTER SIXTEEN

———

I stared down into the man-sized hole in the top of the aquarium at The Deep Blue. Below me, several schools of colorful fish darted back and forth, happy that something new was occupying the sharks for the time being. I tried my best to keep my meal down as I thought about what that "something new" was.

After I'd answered Alfie's call, Rafe had offered to escort me from the restaurant, but I'd politely declined, telling him Alfie was waiting for me. While I was *still* perfectly capable of crossing the street on my own, the truth was I wasn't sure I wanted to be alone with Rafe at the moment. Was I 100% positive he was a murderer? No. But I wasn't 100% positive he wasn't. And with the way my luck was going, those were odds I didn't want to bet on.

Instead, I'd darted from the restaurant as quickly as I could, pushing through the crowd of people gaping at the scene in the Deep Blue's lobby until Security had escorted me to the sixth floor balcony where Alfie and several other grim-faced guys in suits stood taking in the scene from a bird's eye view.

A man from the Crime Scene Unit in diving gear had just opened the tank's hatch, poised at the edge with a long silver pole that had a sturdy loop at the end. He was obviously ready to pull up whatever had the fish in a frenzy. I switched my gaze to the balcony below me, leaning over the railing a bit for a better vantage point. Officers scoured the area under me, chatting with witnesses, taking notes, cordoning off sections of the 5th floor balcony with crime scene tape. Apparently, that was where the action had taken place.

Alfie broke away from the other suits, approaching me. "How's the knot?" he asked, gesturing to my head.

"I'll live." I waved my hand toward the fish tank. "What do you know about this?"

He looked over the railing, and we watched as the diver pulled the bloated faux Pesci from the water. He flopped on his back on the top of the tank, his wide-eyed, lifeless stare seeming to be directed at me. I ducked my head back, taking in deep breaths.

Alfie's eyes danced with amusement. "First time you ever seen a dead guy?"

I briefly glanced at Joe again, his empty glare seeming to have followed me. "Maybe." I swallowed back the few bites of chicken I'd had earlier that were plotting an escape.

"It's never pretty."

I briefly wondered how many non-pretty corpses Alfie had encountered in his line of work. "How did you find him?" I asked.

"Well, your friend there was caught on our camera in the elevator right after your attack. We followed the footage of him as he left The Royal Palace and headed this way. By the time we got here, he was like that."

I swallowed hard. "Any idea how he got 'like that?'"

"I've been told that witnesses saw him fall off the balcony below us into the tank."

I looked at the railing where we stood. It came up to my armpits. Even if Joe was a good foot taller than I was, there was no way he'd accidentally fall over a balcony like that.

"Yeah, I think he was pushed, too," Alfie said, reading my mind.

"Actually, he was stabbed first," Ryder interjected, catching us both off guard.

I spun to find him standing directly behind me, rocking his casual look again. Shirt sleeves rolled up, tie askew, the top button of his shirt undone. I wondered if it was his after-five look, my mind wandering over just what Ryder did in his off hours. I had a hard time imagining him doing anything but popping up at inopportune times and asking annoying questions.

"That's so?" Alfie asked, the tone in his voice challenging, as if he didn't believe the feds had better informants than he did.

Ryder nodded, unfazed. "It is." He glanced over the railing. "See that laceration there?" He pointed to a gash in the dead guy's side. "Knife wound."

"You sure it wasn't just from the sharks taking a nibble?" Alfie probed.

Shark nibbles. Eww. I took a deep breath, telling that chicken it better stay put if knew what was good for it.

"Nothing is certain until the M.E. checks off on it," Ryder hedged. "But, yeah. Unless the shark was wielding a switchblade, I'm pretty sure it was human inflicted."

"Huh," Alfie said, glancing back down at the body. "Guess he was having a real unlucky night."

"To put it mildly." Ryder paused. "How about you, Alfonso? How has your night been?"

Alfie turned his stare from the body squarely on Ryder. It was his steely, stony-faced stare that made card cheaters quake in their boots and employees run for cover.

But if Ryder was intimidated by it, he didn't flinch.

"Why do you ask, Agent Ryder?" Alfie ground out.

"Seems witnesses said you were asking about our victim."

Alfie shrugged. "I'm a curious guy."

"*Before* he was found," Ryder amended.

Alfie's eyes narrowed. "You charging me with something, pal?"

Ryder paused again, and I had a feeling he kind of wanted to. "No," he finally said. "But I'd advise you to stay away from our crime scene."

"Gladly," Alfie spat back. "Come on, Tessie, let's go."

Alfie moved to grab my arm, but Ryder stopped him. "Actually, I need to talk to Tessie. Alone."

Alfie's gaze bounced from Ryder to me, and back again.

"It's okay," I told him, trying to diffuse the testosterone brewing in the air before the fish tank caught a second victim of the evening. "I'm fine."

Finally Alfie nodded. "Fine. Call me when you're at the penthouse. I'm posting a guard tonight."

Before I could protest that I didn't need an armed guard, he was gone. I let out a breath of relief I hadn't realized I'd been holding.

"Charmer, isn't he?" Ryder observed.

I shrugged. "He's old school. What can you do?"

Ryder's mouth curved into a hint of a smile. One that vanished as his eyes roved my face, honing in on the lump which I was sure was turning several lovely shades of purple. "What happened?"

"Long story." I looked down at the tank. "Involving that guy, I'm afraid."

If his face held concern before, it was downright frightening now. "Tell me," he demanded.

So, I did, filling him in on everything that had happened that evening from my place being ransacked to Alfie following our Joe Pesci impersonating friend.

When I was done, Agent Ryder stared at me for a long moment. Then he did the completely unexpected. He grabbed me in a hug. And not the kind that your Aunt Mildred gives you. This one was soft and fierce all at the same time, the kind where emotion overrides all logical thought and your body reacts all on its own. At least, that's what I told myself as I melted into his embrace, my knees all but giving way beneath me as I inhaled the woodsy scent of his aftershave. Pine. Like the fresh trees outside. With a subtle hint of sandalwood.

I was just letting the scent carry me away to a fantasyland filled with silk sheets and warm boxers when he pulled away, holding me at arms' length as he looked me over from head to toe. "You okay?" he asked.

I nodded. Mostly because I didn't trust myself to speak.

He took a deep breath, ran a hand through his hair making it stand up on end. "Jesus, Tessie, you could have been killed."

He glanced at our dead friend, then back up at me. "You sure Alfie found this guy *after* he fell in the water? 'Cause I might be tempted to give him a nudge over the balcony myself if I knew he did that to you."

I was pretty sure that was the nicest thing he'd ever said to me.

I nodded. "Positive. Look, Alfie's rough around the edges, but he's no killer." I was pretty sure.

"Okay, walk me through it," Ryder said, switching back into his professional mode. "Alfie called you to tell you about this guy. What time was that?"

"I don't know. Not too long ago."

"Where were you?"

"At the Golden Chalice having dinner with Rafe."

Ryder's eyes snapped up to meet mine. "You were on a date?"

"Uh..."

"You were on a date." This time it wasn't a question but a statement, all emotion he might have displayed a minute ago drained from his face. "I thought you said you weren't dating Rafe."

"No, I'm not. I mean, yes, I was, but it was a business date. I mean, business meeting. About the casino. Where he works." I blamed the possible concussion that I was rambling like a kid trying to cover her tracks after getting caught with her hand in the cookie jar.

"Agent Ryder!" a voice yelled from the floor below.

I let out a sigh of relief as he leaned over the railing, praising the guy's timing.

"Yes?" Ryder directed below to a uniformed officer.

"There's something you want to see down here," the guy said. "We've got some shiny material lodged between the paneling."

"Shiny?" I muttered, making my way to the banister. I tugged at Ryder's sleeve. "Weston wears those awful shiny shirts. Like, all the time."

Ryder nodded. "That's what I wanted to tell you. We found Weston's prints on the railing where the vic fell over, too."

I couldn't help just the smallest of smug smiles. "Looks like you've got enough to call Weston in for questioning now."

* * *

Ryder insisted on having one of his officers escort me to the penthouse, where, true to my word, I promptly called Alfie to tell him that he could post his rent-a-goon.

Britton answered the door, her face falling into a frown when she saw me. "Dang, girl. That really is some bump. Come on in. I'll get you an ice pack." Her arm encircled my shoulders, leading me to the couch. Boxes filled the living room, pulling me from obsessing over Rafe, Alfie, Joe Pesci, and the look of utter disappointment on Ryder's face at the mention of my dinner versus the heat still pulsing through my body at the feel of his body pressed to mine. Britton's whole life, and her time with my dad, was shoved into these cardboard containers stacked against the walls and lining the hall.

"I really wish there was something I could do to help."

"With packing?" Britton sat next to me, pushing me back and applying a blue ice pack to my temple.

The cold was a shock at first, but it quickly went to work, easing the pain some. I placed one hand over the pack and waved the other around the room. "I wish I could help this all not suck so much."

She patted my leg. "Hey, I found something while going through Dickie's stuff I think will take your mind off of everything." Britton got up and dug through a box near the front door, returning with a tiny wrapped package. She set it on my lap. "Open it. Your dad got it for your birthday last year, when you said you'd come for a visit."

But I never did.

The room spun a bit, feeling like I was hit on the head all over again. This time the pain radiated in my chest, angry fingers clutching my heart. I'd never thought about the times I had let my father down, the promises *I'd* broken, or the white lies *I'd* told, always so wrapped up in my own disappointment.

I pushed the box back toward Britton. "I can't. I don't deserve anything."

She dropped to her knees in front of me, cradling the box into my palm and wrapping my fingers around it. "He loved you so very much. He was saving this because he knew you'd come out one day."

"For his funeral," I blubbered, tears falling freely.

"Don't be so hard on yourself."

I studied the small gift, carefully wrapped in bright yellow paper, my favorite color. The bow was lopsided and tied too tightly, obviously done by my dad. This tightened the grip in my chest. I gasped for breath, the tears coming even faster. I wanted to preserve the paper, the package, and really didn't even care what was inside. The fact that my father had actually wrapped the gift himself spoke louder than whatever present lay within.

Curiosity finally bested me. I wedged the bow off intact and gently draped it on the table next to me. Slowly peeling back the tape, I was able to save the sunny paper as well. I pulled the top off of the box, exposing a pair of diamond stud earrings, a tiny scrap of paper falling away. I picked it up. Scrawled in his nearly illegible handwriting, it said, "I knew you wouldn't come on your birthday. I'm just glad you finally made it. Love you, kiddo." I pressed the note to my chest, sobbing, wishing my daddy could hug all of the pain away one more time, regretting every wasted vacation and opportunity to come visit. Britton's arms encircled me again, and I drew as much comfort from her as I could.

When I was finally able to curb the crying, Britton whispered, "The guest room is made up for you. Most of your things are in there."

"Thank you for letting me stay with you. I just don't feel safe in my room."

"Don't be silly." She playfully swatted my arm. "I wouldn't have it any other way."

I gently gathered my treasures and took them to my room, splaying them on my nightstand. The room was decent sized with a full bed and its own bathroom off to the side. I dug through my hastily packed suitcase, found some sleep pants and a T-shirt, and quickly changed. As I slid into bed, I was overcome with a sense of peace. I knew I was right where my father wanted me, fighting for his casino, safely under his roof. And sleep claimed me quickly.

For a while.

My ringing phone startled me awake. Swiping it on without looking, I muttered, "Hello?"

"Hey, sorry to wake you," I heard Ryder's voice.

I sat bolt upright, smoothing my hair and straightening my pajamas for some odd reason. "Hi, I'm awake." Now.

"I wanted to be the one to tell you. We had to let Weston go."

"What?!" I shouted. I consciously lowered my voice so I didn't wake Britton, then added, "Why?"

"Weston has video of himself at the casino, time stamped and everything, for the time of the struggle and Leo Cannetti's murder." He breathed a defeated sigh directly into the phone. "We couldn't keep him."

"Leo Cannetti?" My groggy brain tried to keep up.

"Oh, the Joe Pesci guy."

I couldn't believe it. Weston was a sure thing. "What about the fingerprints?"

"It's Weston's casino. His prints are all over it." I could hear the defeat in his voice.

"And the fabric at the scene? Wasn't it from Weston's shirt?"

"Hard to tell," Ryder said. "The crime lab is comparing the two, but it will be awhile before we have anything conclusive. In the meantime, Weston's a free man. Sorry, Tessie," he said, and I had a feeling he truly was.

I hung up and checked the glaring red numbers of my alarm clock telling me that everyone else was sound asleep. First sign of sunlight, I was chatting with Weston myself. I, for one, didn't need a warrant.

# CHAPTER SEVENTEEN

———

After the phone call from Ryder in the wee hours of the morning, I'd accomplished nothing more than tossing and turning until I knew the Java Joust was open for business. I'd grabbed a quick shower, then thrown on a pair of grey slacks and my white blouse. (Which had miraculously been cleaned by the very efficient penthouse staff. If I wasn't careful I could really get used to someone else doing my laundry.) I needed to be out of the penthouse before Britton woke and wanted to tag along. There was no way that woman could keep her cool around Weston, and cool was one thing this interrogation was going to require. I mindlessly turned my new earrings in my lobes as I slammed shots of espresso and people-watched. Early risers shuffled through the lobby, entirely too cheery and bubbly for the time of day. Tate's voice caught my attention, rising above the hum of conversation.

I finished my drink and popped a mint into my mouth before walking out into the lobby to find him. I had expected to see him behind the desk. Instead, he was leaning against the wall by the elevators talking to three women in employee uniforms.

He caught my eye as I approached. Then he clutched his chest and gave me a wide-eyed stare. "Well, Tessie King, as I live and breathe. You do know it's not even eight in the morning, right? What are you doing up with the roosters, girl?"

"Ha. Ha. Very funny," I said, joining him. As a teenager, I hadn't particularly been known for being a morning person. Truth be told, I'd been more of a crack-of-noon person. In my defense, I'd been a teenager.

"I was just telling these ladies about my Michael," Tate said, then released a heady sigh, his eyes glistening with that far off, dreamy look.

"Pick out a china pattern yet?" I teased.

"Practically," one employee, a short red-haired girl, said. "He's making us all jealous."

"Hey, don't hate on a playah," Tate piped up.

Which resulted in a round of giggles from his posse, before the red-haired girl checked her phone. "Dang, I gotta get back to the front desk. Call me later, Tate," she said as she and the other women wandered off to their respective posts. I'd like to think it was because my employees were all so punctual, though a small part of me wondered if hanging with the boss didn't make them nervous.

"So, seriously," Tate said. "What act of God propelled you from bed before lunch?"

"Agent Ryder called me last night."

Tate squealed. "Ohemgee, Tessie, I knew you were holding out on me with that hottie."

I shook my head and waved a hand between us. "No, not even close to being that kind of call." I filled him in on the details of Weston, his almost arrest, and subsequent release. "He has to be in on it all. I mean, it's too coincidental for him not to be. I saw him handing off a payment to those two guys. And I plan to find out why."

Tate pursed his lips, his eyes narrowing.

"What?" I asked.

"I don't think this is such a hot idea, Tessie. I mean, you were *attacked* last night," he said, emphasizing the word with drama worthy of a Broadway stage.

"Weston isn't going to attack me in broad daylight."

"Honey, Weston doesn't go into broad daylight. He stays in his casino cave with the other slimy insects."

"Wow, you have about the same love for him that Britton does," I observed.

Tate wrinkled up his nose. "After talking to Michael, yes, I do. He says, Weston makes them work overtime, then fudges their time cards so he doesn't have to pay extra. And he skimps on everything from health insurance to TP in the men's bathroom."

"Jerk."

"I know, right!"

"Which is all the more reason to think he's involved."

But Tate shook his head vehemently from side to side. "No way, honey. It's all the more reason to leave this to Agent Hottie Pants and keep yourself out of harm's way."

I blinked at him. "Wow, really? I expected you to be the last man in my life trying to play macho and send me to the spa."

Tate's forehead wrinkled. "Not that a spa day doesn't sound divine, but there is nothing here being macho," he said, running a hand over his skin tight slacks.

I had to stifle a giggle. He was so right.

"I just don't want to see you get hurt," Tate concluded.

"I know. Sorry, overreaction. I've just had it up to here with the old boy's club around here."

"Welcome to casino life," Tate mumbled. "But seriously, if you are set on going to talk to Weston...I'll go with you. I'll be your bodyguard." He puffed out his chest and widened his stance, trying to pull off a menacing look. I didn't have the heart to tell him it just made him look constipated.

"Thanks," I told him.

"And, if we need backup, I can call Michael. I have him on my favorites list." Tate shoved his phone in my face as though I needed proof he really had Michael's number.

"Sounds like I'm covered, then."

"Wait." Tate put on his wireless phone earpiece, cued up Michael's number, and tucked the phone into his pocket. "Now, all I have to do is push this little button." He hovered a finger over his earpiece and led me out the front doors.

He nodded toward the valets. "'Sup?"

I pushed down his pinky.

Entering the Deep Blue, it was business as usual on the gaming floor. Slots dinged, roulette balls clattered, and the ever-present smoke filled the air in a thin haze. In fact, the only sign that anything sinister had happened here yesterday was the hole in the top of the fish tank and some yellow crime scene tape fluttering on the fifth floor balcony like leftover party streamers.

My eyes scanned the giant tank, unable to see it through a menacing tint now. There were no dead bodies floating, but, from now on, I'd always check.

One of the Deep Blue staff touched Tate's arm. He yelped, pushing the button on his headset.

The clerk turned wide eyes toward me. "I didn't mean to scare you. You just looked lost. Can I help you folks find your room or something?"

Tate frantically shook his head. "No, we are…" Then his eyes lit up as a voice sounded in his ear. Turning toward me, he mouth Michael's name. "Hello, handsome," he cooed, walking over to the aquarium. "Did I wake you?"

So much for my bodyguard.

I smiled at the man in the Deep Blue Casino polo. "I need to speak with Mr. Weston, please."

The pleasant expression faltered for a moment. "Of course. May I ask your name?"

I followed him to concierge desk. "Tessie King. I'm the new owner of the Royal Palace." I expected a glimmer of recognition, but his facial expression remained professionally pleasant.

"I'd be happy to take your contact information down and pass it along to Mr. Weston."

"No, you don't understand. I'd like to *see* him. Now."

"I'm sorry, but Mr. Weston is not taking any meetings today. We've had a bit of a tragedy here," he said, his voice going low as his eyes shot to the aquarium.

I nodded. "I know. That's what I wanted to talk to him about."

"Well, I'm sure he'll be delighted to know that you stopped by, Ms. King. I'll deliver the message to him personally."

I opened my mouth to protest, but I realized it was a lost cause. This guy was polished, professional, and probably a lifer at the Deep Blue. No guest—even the owner of the casino across the street—was going to trump the instructions of his boss.

"Thanks a lot," I mumbled, trying to keep the sarcasm from my voice.

Okay, I didn't try all that hard.

I turned and leaned back against the counter, praying a Plan B came to me.

Tate was still circling the aquarium, his cheeks pink, his eyes bright, his hands waving in the air as he talked. Ah, young love. To his right was a bank of glass elevators. I followed the line of their travel upward. The first six floors of the casino were built atrium style, while the top tower rooms were more private—the suites where the high rollers stayed. If I had to take a guess, I'd say Weston occupied the penthouse, just as my father had.

The only obstacle to getting there would be the hotel security. Currently a pair of guards stood sentinel next to the elevators. I guessed they were supposed to make the guests feel safe staying here despite the crime scene tape. Or keep unwanted nosey reporters (and rival casino owners) away from Weston.

Though, as I recognized one of them as the same guy from the other night at the club, Plan B started to form.

I made my way over to Tate.

"...ohmigod, I love those, too. It's, like, uncanny how much we have in common." He looked up and saw me. I made a wrap it up motion with one hand, and he nodded. "Okay, well, again, so sorry to call so early, but, yes, let's totally do lunch." He paused, listening to Michael on the other end. Whatever he said, it must have been good as Tate blushed like a school girl and giggled. "I can't wait," he squealed. "Ciao!" He pushed a button on his earpiece, then sighed, fanning his face with one hand. "Whew, I think I'm in love."

I couldn't help but grin. "Well, look sharp, loverboy, 'cause I need your help."

He cleared his throat. "Okay, right. I'm in. What do you need?"

"A distraction."

Tate frowned. "What kind of distraction?"

"One big enough to get the attention of those guys over there," I said, gesturing to the two security guards by the elevators. "I need to get to Weston in the penthouse."

Tate groaned, rolling his eyes. "The things I do for you, girl."

I clasped my hands in front of me. "Pretty please, Tate!"

He waved my begging away. "Yes, yes, of course I'll do it. Just give me a minute to prepare."

I gave him a kiss on the cheek. "Thanks!" I called, leaving him in the lobby as I made my way to the gift shop near the elevators. I pretended to scan the magazine rack as I kept one eye on Tate and one on the security duo.

Tate did some pacing, some lip pursing, obviously trying to come up with the perfect plan. Finally he looked up at the huge tank and screamed a blood-curdling, high-pitched thing that had every head in the casino turning his way.

"Oh my God, there's another body in the tank!" He clutched his chest with one hand, pointing up at the blue waters with the other.

That did it.

Obviously dead floating bodies were a touchy subject for Security at the moment, as both guys bolted forward, rushing to Tate's side to scan the tank. Ditto the front desk staff, the concierge, and half the patrons of the casino, some with poker cards still clutched in their hands.

"Where is it?" the security guy from the club asked.

"There!" Tate cried. "At least, I think it was there. Wait, maybe it was just a shark. You know, they look an awful lot like floating people sometimes..."

I didn't waste any time, quickly bolting toward the elevators, stabbing the up button, and waiting an impatient five-count before the carriage arrived and the doors opened. I quickly stepped inside, saying a silent thank you that it was empty, and hit the penthouse button.

My heart was hammering so hard in my chest by the time the doors opened to the penthouse that I thought it might pound right out. I tried to slow my breathing, tell myself I was cool, calm, and in control. When in reality I knew I was going unarmed into a possible murderer's private suite where his team of security could probably make me disappear faster than a guy's paycheck at the slot machines.

I stared at the double doors to Weston's private lair, my finger itching to hit the down button again and scrap this whole mission. I mean, did I really need to talk to Weston *that* badly?

But muffled voices from inside the suite propelled me forward. I tiptoed closer and pressed my ear to the door, but the voices stopped. I backed up at the sound of the lock turning.

Weston cracked the door, wearing a satiny robe and a befuddled look on his face. I prayed there were pajamas underneath. "You do realize there are cameras trained on the door with a monitor here, right?" He pointed next to him inside his room.

"Uh, yeah," I stammered. I did now.

He grunted but opened the door, revealing a very well-dressed man sitting behind him on an upholstered sofa. "What do you want?" Weston asked.

I licked my lips. I didn't think asking for a confession straight up was going to get me anywhere. "I wanted to talk. About my dad."

Weston snorted. "Sorry, honey, but this ain't free therapy. You want a trip down memory lane, go talk to that stacked step-mother of yours."

I looked behind him. The well-dressed guy was sizing me up, eyes narrowed, stare level and assessing, hand hovering near a tell-tale bulge at his side.

I swallowed hard. "Okay, then let's talk about Brad Dunley. And Leo Cannetti. And Johnny Smith. Though I'm pretty sure that last name was a fake."

Weston's eyes narrowed, his jaw set in a tense line. "You're right," he spat out. "It sounds like we do need to talk."

I wasn't sure if I was relieved or more nervous as Weston stepped aside to let me into his penthouse. I felt cold shivers trail up my spine as he locked the door behind me and his well-dressed friend rose from the sofa. I tried to shake the feeling off, gathering what courage I had left as I faced Weston.

"I saw you giving them money. Now two are missing, and one is dead."

"Goody for you. You can do math," he said, heavy on the sarcasm.

"I think you killed him," I challenged, surprised at how steady my voice came out considering my insides were total jelly.

"Like I give a shit what you think," he spat back.

"Agent Ryder thinks you killed him, too." I had one eye on Weston, one on his goon who was hovering near the window, hand still loose over that bulge.

"Agent Ryder has no proof," Weston told me, sitting on the sofa and crossing one ankle onto the other knee. I was very relieved to see that he had sleep pants on under his robe.

"Not *yet*."

Weston smiled. "You're assuming there is proof, dollface." He spread his hands wide. "But I'm an innocent man."

I channeled my dad as I prepared to do my best bluff. "Innocent or not, you're going to have Agent Ryder and the rest of the Nevada Organized Crime Task Force crawling all over your casino for months to come. He's not a man who gives up easily. Trust me—the Royal Palace has been his second home for the past week."

Weston's jaw tensed again at that, some of his smile fading.

"Of course," I continued, shrugging, "I guess I should be thanking you. Since Mr. Cannetti decided to take a swim in your tank, Ryder's vacated the Royal Palace. Things are back to normal now. In fact, I heard business doubled overnight." I paused. "Huh, I wonder if some of those sales were from your guests, switching casinos."

Weston's face was practically contorted into a sneer now, his entire body tense. "All right, what do you want?"

"The truth," I told him, sitting on a hard-backed chair across from him. "Why were you paying off Cannetti and the valet?"

Weston glanced at the well-dressed guy. He gave the barest of nods in agreement. Then Weston turned back to me and took in a deep breath. "I was paying for information."

"What kind of information?" I pressed.

"About a thief at the Royal Palace."

That stopped me. I'd assumed that Weston was the thief. "Wait—you didn't know anything about the thefts?"

Weston uncrossed his legs and leaned forward, both elbows on his thighs. "Look, about a month ago this guy Cannetti comes to me and says he's got some info. He knows something about a scheme at the Royal Palace so big that the scandal would take the whole place down. He wants to know if I'm interested in buying that info. So I says, 'hell, yeah, I am.'"

"So you paid Cannetti to find out what the scheme was?"

Weston nodded. "But the bastard was spoon feeding me information, asking for more money each time we met. He told me they were stealing from guests. They had a crew organized, knew how to block out security footage, and someone on the inside using their pass key. It was all pretty damned genius, I gotta say."

"But Cannetti wasn't the one organizing it."

Weston shook his head. "Nope. That was the kicker. Cannetti said once everyone found out who was behind it, it would take the casino down for sure. Finally I told him I was giving him one more payment, and I wanted to know everything—including who this guy was—or I was gonna break his knees."

I raised an eyebrow his way. "So, you threatened the guy who turned up dead in your fish tank."

Weston put his hands up in a surrender motion. "Hey, he didn't have no broken knees, did he?"

I had to give him that one. "Okay, so what happened? Did Cannetti agree to tell you who was behind it all?"

Weston nodded. "Yeah. That payment you saw at the lounge was the last one. He was supposed to get this guy on tape, setting up the next heist. Irrefutable proof."

"So who was it?" I asked. I was on the edge of my seat now, dying to know.

But Weston sat back, crossing his legs again as he shrugged. "No idea. I was supposed to meet him to get the evidence yesterday."

"That's why he was at the Deep Blue."

Weston nodded. "I was supposed to meet him on the fifth floor balcony. But when I got there, he was already..."

"...swimming with the fishes. That's why your prints were there," I said, thinking out loud.

He raised an eyebrow at me. "You know, my security guy said you were friendly with the cops."

"Feds," I corrected, automatically.

Weston shook his head. "You're in town, what? Four days? And already you're ratting to the organized crime dopes."

"Hey, Ryder is not a dope." Though why the hell I was defending him I had no idea. "And I'm not ratting. I'm...trying to find out what happened to my dad."

Weston leaned forward again, his eyes intent on mine. "Look, whatever happened to your dad's got nothin' to do with me. I wanted to take the man down. But I didn't take him out. I had more respect for the guy than that."

As much as I hated Weston, I was inclined to believe him. Everything he said fit too well. And he had zero tells going on. "Cannetti didn't give you any indication who might be behind the thefts?" I grasped.

Weston shook his head. But then he paused, something warring behind his eyes. "Look, I'm not sure I should say anything, what with your dad being, you know, deceased and all."

Yeah, I knew. "What? Tell me."

Weston chewed the inside of his cheek. But finally he spilled it. "Cannetti mentioned something. Before Richard died. Honestly, I thought your dad was gonna turn out to be the guy behind the thefts."

"Why would you think that?" I asked.

"Cannetti. He was vague, but he said he'd seen wise guys at the Palace. That their connections went all the way to the top."

I looked at him from the corner of my eye. "What do you mean, 'the top?'" I asked, even though I knew how he was going to answer.

"Your dad."

I refused to believe it. "My dad was *not* in with the mob, and he was *not* crooked." But even as I said it, I thought back to my first meeting with Agent Ryder. He'd said the same thing, that he'd been looking into something fishy at the helm of the casino for months.

"Believe what you want, toots. I'm just sayin' what I heard."

I shoved my doubts down, shaking my head. "Cannetti was probably just lying to get a bigger payday from you," I protested.

"Well, Cannetti ain't talking no more, so your guess is as good as mine. That's all I know." Weston folded his arms across his chest and set his jaw, classic signals that he was done being hospitable.

With one last glance at his hired goon, I stood and quickly slipped out the door.

As I waited for the elevator, my mind reeled over all that Weston had told me. Britton and I had been right about the thefts. We'd just had the wrong bad guy at the helm. So, who was it? Weston said it was someone inside the Palace—someone connected enough to the casino to take the whole place down with them if it became public. I felt my skin prickle at the thought, my suspicions about Rafe flooding back. He was certainly a public figure, and his name was almost synonymous with the casino. Could he really be behind it all? And, if so, why? It wasn't as if he needed the money.

And then there was Britton. I'd felt horrible about suspecting her before...but there was someone who *did* need the money. If Britton knew my dad was leveraged to the hilt, she could have organized the thefts to put aside a little nest egg of her own. As much as I wanted to believe everything about her, the truth was I wanted to believe *everyone* at the Palace was loyal to my father and as clean as anyone in the casino business could be. I couldn't see anyone there hurting a fly.

I bit my lip. Except Alfie. If anyone had a shady past, it was that guy. He'd been my father's right hand man for as long as I could remember...but who better to have access than Alfie? It would have been the easiest thing in the world for him to "lose" security footage when the thefts occurred. And no one was more inside than the head of security.

My phone ringing from my pocket startled me out of my thoughts so badly I nearly peed my pants. Britton's face filled my screen, and I took a deep breath before answering and stepping into the elevator.

"Hello?"

"Tessie, you have to come up here right away!" Her voice was loud, breathless, and held a hint of hysteria.

"What's wrong?"

"The Vermeer... It's gone!"

# CHAPTER EIGHTEEN

———

I sat on the couch with Britton, holding one of her hands, as we watched the police once again search her things. Part of the gesture was to comfort her, the other part to keep her from assaulting the officers.

"Be careful!" she yelled, yanking against my grip. "That box is full of fragile things." She turned sad eyes toward me. "Please, make them stop. I'm so tired of all this."

"I know. Me, too," I agree wholeheartedly.

As soon as I'd gotten her call, I'd gone straight to the penthouse, only to find a crew of police officers once again going through Britton's personal belongings. While no one would actually talk to me to give me a straight story, the general consensus seemed to be that the police thought Britton had slipped the painting into a suitcase as a "parting gift," then called in the theft as a ruse. I'd left three voicemails for Agent Ryder, but so far he'd yet to make an appearance at the scene.

Instead, I watched as Alfie walked through the penthouse doors. His suit was rumpled, his jaw tense, his expression sour. "Tessie," he barked. Then he waggled a finger, summoning Britton and me into the hall, out of the earshot of the grabby-hands officers.

I followed his lead. "Did you find anything?" I asked, my voice more hopeful than I felt.

Alfie shook his head grimly. "I'm afraid not. Between the time Britton left for the gym and Ellie came in to clean, the place was only empty for roughly twenty minutes. We cued up all the security footage we had during that time frame."

"And?" Britton asked, the desperation in her voice rising into squeaking Minnie Mouse territory.

"Let me guess, the footage hiccupped again?" I supplied.

"Even worse," Alfie said. "The feed for the whole top five floors was wiped, and then there were random floors with missing blips. There isn't even a way to track where the painting went after it left here."

"The insider," I mumbled. He didn't need Cannetti or his other crew for this one. He fixed the footage, waltzed in, and took the painting all on his own. My eyes bounced from Alfie to Britton. So, who was the insider man? Or woman?

But Alfie shook his head. "No. This isn't related to the other thefts. The M.O. is completely different than any of the other incidents."

I gaped at him. "How can you say that? You really think it's just coincidence?"

Alfie shot me a look. "I think it's a stolen painting, and we'll track the guy who took it and get it back. Beyond that, I don't make up stories about why he stole it."

I rolled my eyes. "They're called *theories*, not stories."

"Well, in my book, they're the same thing. And they get us nowhere."

Britton put a calming hand on Alfie's arm. "Just find whoever did this, please. I can't live under this cloud of suspicion any longer."

Alfie nodded. "I'll go run the feed from the other floors and see if we can find something. At this point, we're searching for a snowflake in a blizzard. Don't get your hopes up."

With that, he stormed out of the penthouse.

But as I watched him retreating, I had to admit he was right about one thing. The M.O. *was* completely different. But even more different was the stolen item. Carvell's stolen cash was completely untraceable, easy to spend. The diamond necklace might be less so, but they could have broken it down and sold off the diamonds individually without too many raised eyebrows. The Vermeer was different. It was a one of a kind, priceless work of art. There's no way the thief could unload it without being outed. So, why steal it to begin with?

To frame Britton, perhaps? Was someone feeling the heat a bit too much? She would be the perfect, clueless scapegoat.

An officer tapped Britton on the shoulder. "Mrs. King, we need to ask you some questions."

"I already answered your stupid questions with him." Her hand shot out, pointing at a different officer digging through her packed lingerie in the hallway. "And, just for the record, I doubt anyone could fit the painting in that small of a box between pairs of panties!" she yelled, stomping toward the man in question.

I darted behind her, grabbing her arm just as she geared up to smack him away from her unmentionables. "Let's go to the Minstrel Lounge for a drink before they add assaulting an officer to your list," I whispered in her ear.

Turning toward me, face beet red, she muttered, "It's only noon."

"You know the saying. It's five o'clock somewhere." I forced a playful smile to my face. "We'll have a salad, too."

"Okay."

I pulled her toward the door, stopping at the officer standing guard. "We'll stay on casino property. You have our numbers."

He looked at the lead officer and nodded.

* * *

The same goateed host was on duty at the Minstrel Lounge. Menus in tow, he scurried to us.

"Mrs. King, Ms. King, what a pleasure!" he cried. "Right this way. The best seat in the house for you ladies." He led us to the same table Tate and I had shared. As we sat, I glanced out at the scenery. The daytime view of the mountains was just as breathtaking as the evening. I suddenly longed to be out there, feeling the crisp cool air on my face, boarding down the mountain at a breakneck speed, leaving all the questions and suspicions behind.

"Can I bring you ladies something to drink?"

"Whiskey sour," Britton mumbled, elbows on the table, her face buried in her hands.

The host's eyes rounded a bit before he turned to me. "And for you?"

"I'll have what she's having, and add a couple of house salads, too."

Britton peered at me through her fingers. "I'm not really hungry."

"It's a salad. I'm willing to bet you haven't eaten anything today with all that's been going on."

"Yeah." She nodded, dropping her hands to the table, rattling the place settings in the process. "This has been one of the worst days ever. They basically accused me of taking the painting. It's bad enough that everyone thinks I killed my Dickie, but to steal from him, too? Please."

I reached across the table and patted her hand. "I know you didn't kill my father, if that helps any."

"That means the world to me right now. You know I didn't steal the painting, too, right?" Her eyes held a child-like innocence, begging me to believe in her.

And in that moment, I totally did. No one could lie that well without giving something away. And Britton was nothing if not genuine. I felt guilty all over again for suspecting her to have anything to do with the thefts.

"Of course," I told her, taking a large gulp of my drink as soon as the server appeared with it. It was strong, but didn't do much to wash the guilty feeling away.

As our salads were set in front of us my phone vibrated in my pocket. I glanced down as I pulled it out. Rafe's face smiled up at me.

I paused, finger hovering over the "on" button. With guilt warring with suspicion, warring with the knowledge that at least one person I trusted had killed my dad, I didn't trust myself to pick up. I let the call go to voicemail, taking another sip of my drink instead.

"Who was that?" Britton asked.

I shoved a forkful of lettuce into my mouth to keep from answering, offering her a languid shrug instead. After swallowing, I asked as casually as I could, "What do you know about Rafe? I'm only familiar with the man on the mountain, you know."

"Ah." She set her fork down and took a long sip of her drink. "The date didn't go so well, eh?"

"It as a business meeting."

"Sure, whatever you say." Her words agreed with me, but the lopsided grin said otherwise. "What do you want to know?"

I glanced at the poster of him and his Barbie clone manager. While asking about their relationship was on the tip of my tongue, I asked instead, "What do you know about his life pre-fame?"

Britton pursed her lips, getting a far off look in her eyes as if recalling some conversation from the past. "Did you know he was raised in foster homes?"

I shook my head. "No. I had no idea."

She nodded. "Yeah, pretty much all his life. He said snowboarding was a way to get away from the system, so he threw himself into it, heart and soul." She took another drink, casting a thoughtful gaze out the window. "He said your dad gave him his first board. It was some sort of Christmas charity drive for foster kids, you know? Dickie was always doing stuff like that for the local community. Anyway, I guess Rafe really took to it."

This was all news to me. I guess I'd known my dad gave to charity, but I hadn't realized he'd been so hands on about it. I'd always imagined him just writing a check in his office when tax time came around. "How did Rafe end up here?" I asked.

"I'm not entirely sure how he ended up at the Royal Palace. I do know he was a stubborn prick when he first started out, totally out for himself. He had a really bad rep on the mountain for awhile. But Dickie helped him get his start here. I think Rafe kind of saw him as a father figure, you know? He's had several opportunities to take off to Aspen or Vail or, heck, even Europe. But he turned them all down."

"Why?"

"He told me family meant the world to him, and this was the closest thing he'd ever had."

I digested that while I sipped my drink again. I was just starting to feel a warm glow in my belly when my phone rang again.

Expecting it to be Rafe again, I answered without looking. "Hey, you."

"Uh, hey yourself, Ms. King," Stintner said, with an uneasy laugh.

I felt my cheek flush. "Oh, I'm sorry. The last call was...well, never mind. What can I do for you?"

"I have some insurance claim forms that need to be filed as soon as possible. You'll need to sign off on them as chairman."

"How long will it take?" I asked, glancing across at Britton.

I heard him shuffle through papers. "Only a few minutes. If you can come up now, I've got them all ready."

I nodded. "I'll be right there, then." I hung up and explained the situation to Britton. "I'll be right back, though." Finishing my drink, I waved as I darted out the door.

I arrived at Stintner's suite to find him waiting at the front desk for me. "My secretary is off today. Come on back."

I followed him into his office and sat across his polished desk from him. He slid a stack of documents to me, all opened to the pages with sticky arrows on them, showing me where to sign. I contemplated reading through everything, but even the small amount of legalese on the pages showing made my head hurt. And the whiskey sour wasn't helping. I stared up at him, mindlessly spinning my earring again, contemplating my position with the casino and what might be expected in this situation.

"These are the claims for theft from Carvell's room and the diamond necklace from Mrs. Ditmeyer's," he explained, clearly reading my nervousness at being in over my head.

I smiled at him. "Thanks. I just sign here?"

He nodded. "I've filled in all the appropriate amounts, attached all the documentation, and filled out the forms. Your signature is all we need to file, and we should see a check for compensation in the next two to three weeks."

"Which goes to the guests?"

Stintner nodded again. "Correct."

"What about the Vermeer?" I asked, signing my name next to the first arrow.

"Ah. Right. Alfie informed me of that tragic loss," he said. "The painting was insured separately by the hotel as their property. I should have that paperwork drawn up for you to sign before the board meeting."

He smiled at me as he flipped each document closed and straightened them into a neat pile. "Thank you so much for taking care of this so quickly. It must be in your genes." His face grew somber, gaze falling to his hands. "Your father was always willing to drop everything when I needed him."

I stood and reached a hand toward him. He looked back up, the smile returning to his face and shook it. "I'll escort you to the elevator."

I waved him off, backing toward the door. "I'll be fine, thanks."

As I left his offices and took the elevator back down to Britton, my thoughts turned to the Vermeer again. While the other thefts had felt like a blow to the casino, this one somehow felt more personal. I would have killed to have a piece like that in my gallery. I could only hope the thief was taking proper care of it. I itched to call Alfie and ask if he'd had any more luck with the footage, but I knew if he had, he would have called me already.

I silently wondered if the painting was still in the hotel. I mean, it wasn't like anyone could just walk out of the casino with a package the size of that painting without someone noticing. Then again looking for it here was like finding a needle in a haystack. It wasn't like Alfie could conduct a room-to-room search without upsetting every single guest of the hotel. Or alerting them to the fact that a thief was amongst them. But if it still was here, then maybe we'd have a chance of catching the thief as he tried to smuggle it out. As I crossed back into the Minstrel's Lounge, I made a mental note to tell Alfie to post more security near the exits, just in case.

I was pleasantly surprised to see Tate had joined Britton at our table. "Hey, girlfriend!" he called, his voice cutting through the idle chatter at the other tables, garnering their attention as well.

Business had picked up, with almost every table now full. I wound my way through the lunch crowd toward them, noticing that not only had Britton finished her salad, but there were now two empty glasses sitting next to her.

Tate scooted toward the window, patting the bench next to him. "I heard through the grapevine you and Britton were having lunch up here. I simply had to know how the Weston meeting went and what the hell happened to the painting. So, this is where I'm spending my lunch hour. Curiosity isn't just a danger to cats, you know."

I slid in next to him and caught him up to speed on the issues currently 'endangering' him. When I was done, I asked, "So, if you had to guess, how would someone manage to get a package that big out the door?"

He shrugged. "I don't know. But I can tell you that Alfie has extra security posted at the front door and near the check-out desk."

I scratched out my mental note. Apparently my head of security was one step ahead of me. A thought that *should* have made me glad, but instead left me feeling kind of useless.

"Trust me," Tate added, seeing my face fall, "if that painting is still here, it isn't leaving this building."

"Thanks, Tate."

He smiled back at me. Then his face instantly morphed into a look of panic. "Oh, honey." His eyes scanned from one side of my face to the other. "One of your earrings is gone."

My fingers flew to my ears, and sure enough, the right one was bare. "My dad bought those for me." I felt sick.

Britton's face mirrored Tate's concern. Or, attempted to through the Botox. "When did you last have them both?"

I bit my lip. "I don't know. I mean...they were here when I was with you, right?" I asked her.

Britton nodded. "I think so?" She looked down at her empty glasses. "But I'm not sure. I've had a little bit to drink." She punctuated that statement with a hiccup, which she tried to daintily cover in one manicured hand.

I nodded. "No, I think you're right," I said, remembering how I'd fiddled nervously with it in Stintner's office. "I'm going to backtrack to see if I can find it," I said, sliding from the table.

"Want me to help?" Britton asked, standing also. Well, trying to stand. As soon as she stood her legs wobbled, and her hand shot out to catch herself on the table.

"Uh, maybe you should go lie down for a bit," Tate suggested instead.

Britton nodded. Then her eyes welled up. "But I can't go to the penthouse. The police are all over it."

"No worries, honey," Tate told her, steering her gently toward the door. "I can set you up in a room until they're done." He sent me a wink over his shoulder, and I had complete confidence that Britton was in good hands.

Myself, I made a bee-line for the elevators, scanning every inch of carpet along the way. Ditto the elevator tile as I made my way to Stintner's office again. When I got there, my heart fell to see all of the lights off. I tried the door and, thankfully, it swung open.

"Mr. Stintner?" I called out as I walked inside.

I scanned the flooring in the lobby, using my phone for light as I made my way down the hall toward his office. Luckily the light switch was easier to find here. Overhead fluorescents immediately illuminating the room. I checked around the chair I'd sat in, and then ran my hands over the desktop. I was just about to start to panic when I saw a glint of something shiny tucked between two papers. I dove for it, almost crying out in relief when my hands clutched around my earring. The back was nowhere to be found, but the important part was now slid into my pocket.

I looked down at the papers it had been wedged between. The forms I'd just signed. Only the earring was lodged into a page I hadn't looked at—one without a sticky arrow. I felt a frown pull between my eyebrows as I glanced at it. It was the page stating the value of the loss the hotel had sustained, just like Stintner had promised. Carvell's name was on it, the value of the theft easy to calculate as it had all been in cash. But in the box where the dollar amount was supposed to be, someone had filled it in to read $15,000. I slid the paper closer. There had only been $5,000 in Carvell's safe. Vaguely I wondered if Mary Beth had made some sort of clerical mistake as I shuffled through to the next stack of papers, the claim for the diamond necklace. Only this one seemed to have increased as well.

As I stared at the papers, my mind swirled, puzzle pieces magically clicking into place in perfect unison. Why the diamond necklace, why the Vermeer. It was never about the items themselves. It was about the insurance. And I was pretty sure I knew who had insured everything.

"Hello, Tessie," I heard his voice coming from the doorway.

I turned slowly to find Stintner watching me, his eyes sharp, his voice calm, and his hand gripped around a pistol aimed right at my forehead.

# CHAPTER NINETEEN

———

I held my hands out toward the gun. "Mr. Stintner, what are you doing?"

"Me?" he said calmly. "I believe you are the one trespassing."

Pointing at my pants pocket, I forced an innocent look to my face. "I just came back to get the earring I lost. I knocked, and yelled to let you know I was here."

His eyes narrowed, still staring at me over the gun barrel. "And that justifies your actions?"

"My dad bought me the earrings," I continued babbling, hoping to convince him that I hadn't seen the documents. "They were supposed to be for my birthday. I just didn't want to lose one of them. They mean so much to me."

He looked past me at the desk and disheveled papers. "Nice try. I see you were digging through the insurance documents. Find anything that interested you?"

"No." I shook my head emphatically. "I swear."

"It isn't nice to lie to your elders." His expression softened a bit. "I watched you grow up, Tessie. It shouldn't have had to end this way."

"What way? Please, Mr. Stintner," I said, hearing the desperation in my own voice. My mind was numb, unable to come up with any sort of escape route, all attention focused on the gun pointed at me.

"I'm sorry, Tessie," he said, shaking his head as if he really were.

"Wait! What are you talking about?" I tried to play dumb and stay calm, but panic blazed through every cell in my body.

"You aren't stupid, Tessie. More importantly, I'm not stupid."

Dammit. I swallowed hard, looking left and right. There was only one way out of the room, and Stintner was blocking it. I glanced above myself at the ceiling. It was one of the few places not graced with black security cameras. I cursed attorney client privilege as my mind raced for some way to get out. I needed more time. I needed to stall him.

"Okay, look, yes, I...I'm not that dumb," I said.

"Obviously," he observed, dryly.

"I know it was you who orchestrated the thefts, wasn't it?" I asked, trying to appeal to his ego. "You were the genius behind the scheme?"

At this, a small smile quirked the corner of his mouth. "It *was* genius. I mean, who ever reads the entire fifteen pages of an insurance claim?"

I'll admit, I hadn't.

"All I had to do was inflate the claims a little, and pocket the cash," he continued. "All the checks were drawn out to the company account where I was a signer. No one noticed, no one questioned."

"But these sorts of claims are few and far between normally," I prompted, keeping him talking.

He nodded. "Normally, yes."

"So, you found a way to create more."

"It was so simple, really. I was surprised no one else had thought of it before," he bragged. "One day I overheard the valet talking about a whale he'd seen come in with cash for a high-stakes game. I realized he saw *everything* that came into our casino. So, I paid him to keep me informed when a high roller was checking in with extra cash on hand. As soon as they hit the tables, I'd let myself into their rooms and helped myself to the contents of their bags. Just one every now and again, nothing to raise any suspicions or scare anyone off." He paused. "Then I met Mr. Dunley. This is, if you think about it, his fault." Caught in thought, he looked down for a few seconds.

I took the opportunity to close the gap between myself and the door by a few steps. Stintner's eyes shot up.

I froze.

"Uh, Dunely? How is everything his fault?"

Stintner blinked, pulling himself back to present. "He told me he could help grow the payout. Get the whales to order in more cash. He said he'd done it before in Vegas. I gave him a shot with a percentage of the payout. Then he said he needed to bring in Cannetti in order to get the safes open. Fine by me. I just got to sit back and collect the cash. It was a perfect scheme—get paid once from stealing the cash, then get paid again through the insurance company."

I was only half listening at this point, trying to remember how many other doors were in the hall outside his office. Storage? Stairwell? Emergency exit? There were at least three, maybe four. I inched a bit closer to the door. "How did you get the security footage shut down?"

He snorted. "That was thanks to your dear old dad. He gave me his login information once."

"Once? Don't they change that often?"

"Yes, they do, but once was all I needed. I had a hacker set up a ghost login for me. It was expensive, but it's paid for itself several times over, and no one even knew I was in there." He tossed his head back to laugh.

Which explained why Alfie hadn't been looking into him. I inched closer.

"What I don't get is why?" I said, calculating just how quickly I could dive for the doorway versus how quickly his finger could pull a trigger. I wasn't sure I was a fan of the odds.

Stintner blinked at me as if I was an idiot. "For the money, of course. You think I'm stupid?"

"Uh...no?" And even if I did, I certainly wasn't going to say that to the guy holding a gun on me.

"Of course not. I knew every aspect of your father's business. I knew the casino was in trouble. Another year, and your father would have run this place into the ground. I'd be dammed if I was going down on that sinking ship. I gave twenty-five years of service to Richard King. I deserved a payout."

Clearly he was losing his grip on reality. Unfortunately his grip in the gun seemed as strong as ever. I licked my lips, running out of stall techniques. Wasn't there anyone else on this floor? Didn't anyone work around here on a Saturday? A janitor, someone?

"So what happened?" I asked. "If it was all going so well, why stop?"

"Those assholes got greedy," Stintner said, spittle flying from the corner of his mouth as he talked. "Bastards were going to sell me out to Weston. They heard he was trying to take down the Royal Palace while it was vulnerable and mortgaged down to your dad's socks. They turned on me. The traitors!"

Which I found ironic considering he was the one calling the kettle Benedict Arnold.

"So, I had to make some changes in my plans," he continued. "The police and feds were everywhere, you and that blonde bimbo nosing around. It was time for me to retire. I just needed one more score. So, I took the Vermeer from the penthouse. It will look lovely on the walls of my estate in a non-extradition country."

If he wasn't holding a gun on me, I'd have killed him. Instead, I tried to employ some of my mom's yoga breathing to calm my rising anger at the thought of a priceless work of art in the hands of this psycho sleaze. "I suppose your plans also included killing off all of your crew?"

He rolled his shoulders, gaining his composure as he steadied the gun on me. "The valet, yes. I caught him at the end of his shift, then took him for a ride to the lake. Turns out, he couldn't swim. At least not with his hands tied."

I felt my stomach churn over itself, icy goose bumps breaking out on my skin at the thought that "Smith" was now somewhere at the bottom of the crystal blue waters outside the windows.

But if Stintner felt any emotion at the thought of killing a man, he didn't show it. In fact, a small smile curled his upper lip. "That's how we used to do it in the old days, you know. We took care of things *our* way."

"And Dunley?" I took a deep breath, not really wanting to know about the *old* days or the recent ones. But I had to keep him talking.

But Stintner shook his head. "He saw his buddy was missing and took off. Good riddance. He knows what happens to him if he talks."

"He gets killed. Like Smith...and Cannetti."

Stintner grinned in earnest this time, showing off two rows of stained teeth. "That one practically fell into my lap. With one little push I got rid of Cannetti and sent a nice message to Weston as well. I believe that threat will make him think twice."

I blame the fear pumping adrenaline through my system that it wasn't until that moment that it dawned on me. "You sent Cannetti to break into my room. You were threatening me."

Stintner nodded slowly. "I didn't mean for him to hurt you, Tessie. Honest. It was just supposed to scare you."

"It did," I said, meaning it.

"I don't know why you had to go nosing around where it wasn't your business."

I felt my chin rise and before I could stop myself blurted out, "It *is* my business. This is my casino, remember?"

Stintner let out a sharp bark of a laugh. "You are so stubborn. Just like your dad."

I fought back emotion at the mention of him. "You killed him too, didn't you." I swallowed past the bile in my throat at the thought of standing in front of his killer.

This time any smug bragging about his crimes vanished, as a look of true sorrow crossed his features. "He was my friend once, Tess. But the man was so short-sighted. He thought he could run this place just like he always had. Old school. He was running it right into the ground."

"So you killed him for being a bad businessman?" I yelled, feeling anger replace some of my fear.

But Stintner shook his head. "No, I killed him because he was going to find out everything. I never thought it would come to that, I swear!" he said, emotion rising in his voice. His hand was shaking, the gun wagging back and forth at me. "It was my last option. I tried everything to get him off my trail. He just wouldn't let it go!" His grip wavered, trigger finger falling away.

And I realized it was now or never.

I lunged forward, shoving an elbow into his gut, and pushing him to the ground. The gun stayed tight in his hand, but the barrel was now pointed at the ceiling as Stintner tried to regain his footing. I didn't stick around to see if he succeeded, instead flying into the hallway. I tried two doors, both locked, before I heard the gun go off behind me and felt fire erupt in my shoulder, a bullet exploding into the door jamb next to me.

*Ohmigod, I'd been shot!*

I gritted my teeth past the searing pain, diving for the next door and trying the knob. I said a silent thank you that it was unlocked and shoved inside. It was some sort of large archive room, rows of racks filled with file folders in neat rows. I pulled my phone from my pocket, my fingers fumbling as I simultaneously tried to pull up Alfie's number and search for another way out. I was only able to get the number queued before Stintner's keys jingled in the door.

I tore down the middle aisle, and hunched down at the end in the shadows.

"Tessie," I heard Stintner's voice fill the room. "You know I can't let you leave here alive. I'm sorry for everything. There's no way out of this room, and I've got nothing scheduled for the rest of the day. I can wait as long as you can."

I bit my lip, wanting with all my heart to hit send on my phone. But as soon as I did, the light would give me away. I looked up, again seeing a void of cameras. The entire legal department must be without them. Damned things were everywhere until you needed them. I slowly stood, ignoring the pain in my shoulder, trying to remain quiet as I slid along the back wall in the darkness, feeling my way. My fingers grabbed a door handle. I said a silent prayer for another unlocked room as I turned the knob.

Despite not having been to church since I was twelve, my prayers were answered. The door opened easily in my hands. Unfortunately it also creaked on its hinges, instantly giving away my position. Stintner ran toward me, his shadowed features contorted to look like some scary Halloween mask of a mad man.

I slipped into the next room, which I quickly identified as not a room but a supply closet, then slammed the door shut, pushing on it with all my weight. I set my back against the door, bracing with my right leg against the wall, while balancing on my left. Then I pulled my phone back out and pressed send.

"Answer the phone, Alfie, please," I pleaded breathlessly, a death grip on the handle. Only the call dropped. I stared at the bars on my phone, desperation bubbling up in my throat. No reception in the supply closet.

I felt Stintner shove at the door from the other side, jarring my balance. "Tessie, you can't hide forever," he sing-songed.

I fought down a whimper realizing just how far gone he was. I was stuck in a supply closet, bleeding, with a mad man outside the door. I took two deep breaths, feeling Stintner push on the other side of the door again. Come *on, Tessie, keep it together.*

Using the light from my phone, I scanned the room for anything I could shove against the door to bar Stintner's entrance. My legs were quickly giving out. After having re-swiped my phone to life twice, I finally spied an old style rag mop in one corner. I stretched out my good arm, my fingers just grazing the handle. I took a deep breath and stretched again, just as Stintner threw his weight at the door.

I cried out as the wood jarred against my shoulder, but the push gave me the extra inch I needed to reach the mop handle. I spun, wedging it between the square door handle and the corner of the small room, then stepped back taking a moment to breathe again.

"Tess-ie," he sing-songed. "It's only a matter of time before I get you, my dear."

I licked my lips. Not if I could help it.

I scanned the room again, this time looking for anything I could use as a weapon. The room was a hodge-podge of antiquated items—some old winter clothing, abandoned fax machines and Xerox toner, a badminton net with a hole in it, and a broken snowshoe. I tried the weight of the fax machine, but the thing was way heavier than I could lift and throw with any accuracy with my shoulder wound. Snowshoe it would have to be.

I hoisted my make-shift weapon into my hands, watching as Stintner slammed his weight against the door again.

The mop wavered. Another couple of shoves and it wouldn't stand a chance of surviving.

I just hoped that I did.

Taking a deep breath, I mustered all the courage I could, said a prayer that my cat would not end up an orphan, then removed the mop from its wedged spot.

When Stintner's weight came barreling into the door again, it flew open. And I swung the snowshoe at him with all I had, smacking him in the face. His own inertia ratcheted him backwards, falling onto his back on the hard floor. The gun skittered across the concrete floor of the closet as his head made contact with a dull thud. I dove for the gun in the dim light, my fingers clenching around the sweaty grip and turning it on him—even though he looked like he'd clearly been knocked out cold—as I scooted toward the door. I shoved Stinter's prone form into the closet and slammed the door shut. I locked the closet door and set the gun carefully on a shelf. Then I leaned against the wall, afraid my legs had turned to complete mush.

My hands were shaking so badly it took me three tries to pull up Alfie's number again. I could have cried when he finally picked up with a gruff, "Malone?"

"Alfie, have I got a *story* you're going to love."

# CHAPTER TWENTY

———

"Tessie?" Alfie's voice boomed from the hall.

"In here!" I called, afraid to take my eyes off of the room holding Stintner. Alfie burst through the door, flipping on the overhead lights, and I ran into his open arms.

"You're bleeding," he said, holding me tightly. "That bastard shot you?" His jaw clenched, the look in his eyes almost as murderous as Stintner's had been.

I nodded, dropping my head to his chest, soaking up the safety of his strong embrace. "Well, he shot at me. The bullet's in the wall somewhere over there," I said, waving vaguely toward the hallway. "I don't think he's much of a shot." Thank God.

"Where is the sorry son of a bitch?" Alfie ground out.

I pointed to the door with one hand, clinging to him with the other. I wasn't quite ready to stand on my own accord just yet.

"Is he still armed?"

"No, it's on the shelf." I pointed a shaking finger toward it.

Smoothing my hair, he said, "You did good, girl. This could have ended really badly."

I looked up at Alfie, trembling harder at the thought of the alternate ending. "What's going to happen to him?" I asked, not really sure I wanted to know the answer.

Jaw set, temple vein bulging, he muttered, "The man is damn lucky the cops are on their way. Probably best I don't open the door until they get here. Hard to say if there'd be anything left for the cops to arrest."

It didn't take long until the police did arrive, quickly filtering into the room with guns drawn. Alfie pointed toward the locked door, then ushered me out into a nearby office where paramedics arrived a beat behind the officers. Luckily, the bullet just grazed my shoulder, and the paramedic said all I'd need was a few stitches and I'd be as good as new. He quickly dressed the wound in gauze, then gave me a shot of some painkiller that was so nice I could have kissed him.

As he was finishing up, I saw the police escorting a dazed looking Stintner from the back room, parading him down the hallway in handcuffs. I couldn't help but notice the very large, very red snowshoe impression across one side of his face. A giggle escaped me.

Alfie even snickered, clapping a protective hand on my good shoulder. "Your dad would be proud of you. Hell, I'm even proud of you."

I patted my pockets. "You have a pen I can use? This may never happen again. I need to get it in writing."

"Smart ass," he muttered, chucking me on the good shoulder again.

Someone cleared their throat loudly behind me, and I turned to find Agent Ryder standing in the doorway. He nodded toward Alfie. "Can I borrow her for a minute?"

Alfie walked toward him and straightened his tie, cinching it tightly around his neck. "Don't let her wander *anywhere* alone."

I giggled again. (Wow those painkillers were *really* good.) Alfie's tough-guy act was actually kind of cute.

I wasn't sure Agent Ryder shared the same opinion, relaxing his collar as he took a step toward me. His eyes immediately went to the white bandage on my shoulder. "You okay?" he asked.

I nodded. "Bullet just grazed me. I'll be fine. I might have a cool scar to impress the boys with, though," I joked.

But Ryder didn't laugh. Instead, he took a step closer, so close we were almost nose to nose.

Then, without warning, his lips pressed against mine. Minty gum and warm coffee flavors mixed with a rush of hormones to make my head spin. I felt one strong hand cradle the back of my head, the other press against the small of my back as heat spread rapidly through my system, pooling somewhere below my belly button. Just when I thought I was going to melt into a puddle of hormonal goo, Ryder pulled back.

"Wow," I breathed, the room still spinning.

"Sorry," he said, his voice coming out in short pants that matched mine. "But I've been dying to do that for days, now."

I felt the corner of my mouth tick upward. "Really? Days?"

He nodded, a lopsided grin spreading across his face. "Oh, yeah." The grin faltered a little. "And I never would have forgiven myself if I left without doing it."

I blinked. "L-left? Wait—you're going?"

Much to my hormone's disappointment, he nodded. "I've got a case up north I need to take care of."

"Will I see you again?" My voice totally came across needier than I meant it to.

"Oh, I can almost guarantee it." His grin faltered further. "The truth is, Stintner may have been responsible for some of the missing money from the books, and your father's murder. But my original case remains open."

I bit my lip. Right. My father's reported mob connections. Ones that I was having a harder and harder time denying, even to myself.

"Ms. King?" one of the uniformed officers said, poking his head into the room. "We need to get a statement from you."

Ryder nodded toward the officer. "I guess duty calls." And with that, he turned and walked out the door, leaving me feeling surprisingly alone despite the presence of the armed officer.

I touched my lips, emotion and pain killers swirling through my system in a cocktail that left me grinning like a fool though the entire police interview.

* * *

I stood outside the boardroom door, shaking off the remnants of Britton's *harmless* little sleeping pill from hell. While I did indeed sleep, I was finding it hard to focus on the impending emergency board meeting that had been called six days before the scheduled one, in light of Stintner's arrest and the media sensation that was following it. That was one thing Cannetti and crew had been right about—the publicity was *not* good for the casino.

I smoothed my pencil skirt with sweaty palms while I paced the hall. Bittersweet emotions bubbled through me, knowing that the board was behind those doors, discussing the fate of my childhood home. Odd that I thought of it that way now, but after tripping down memory lane for the past few days, I realized that even though I'd lived with my mother 90% of the time, I'd done a lot of growing up within these casino walls.

Walls that might not be standing for much longer.

The door popped open, striking both fear and anticipation through my body simultaneously, and Alfie motioned me in.

Members were seated around a long wooden table, all of them well dressed and somber faced. I was surprised to see Rafe in attendance as well, wearing much the same somber expression as the rest of the assembled group. I fought a wave of guilt at all my prior suspicions about him as I nodded a stiff hello in his direction. He waved a hand in response, but his grim expression didn't change much. Not a good sign.

Alfie escorted me to the end of the table, but instead of sitting, he dropped a gentle hand on my good shoulder.

"Ladies and gentlemen of the board," he said, addressing the room. "You've all had your chances to speak, to tell of your plans to shut this place down, tear it apart, and sell it off piece by piece. The Royal Palace has been my life, and Richard King's life, God rest his soul, for many years. It sickens me to even consider what you're suggesting. I feel, with the right person at the helm, this casino can get back on its feet and return to days of greatness and profit."

I stared up at him, finding myself silently rooting for this anonymous soul Alfie spoke about. I nodded in agreement and turned a confident smile toward the board.

Until Alfie's grip tightened on my shoulder.

"And I think that right person is Ms. Tessie King."

I froze, blinking at the room, wondering if I'd just heard him wrong.

"I'll be beside her every step of the way," Alfie continued, "as she learns the ropes, just like I was with her dad. But the past week, she's shown the sort of gumption that this place needs. No one messes with the Royal Palace while a King is at the helm."

I tried really hard to keep the shock I felt from my face as the board members muttered to one another, all eyes assessing me. While I had been gaining some measure of confidence as the *temporary* leader of this outfit, the idea of doing it permanently had me paralyzed with fear. I would have to give up my life in San Francisco, my artists, the gallery, my apartment. Though, said apartment paled in comparison to the penthouse. Captain Jack would have more room and a nice balcony to sun on.

I bit my lip. Mom was gonna be pissed if I stayed in Tahoe. Probably best to let her know *after* picking up Jack.

Rafe stood and cleared his throat loudly enough to stop the chatter. "I say we give her a chance, perhaps a three month trial period. We can always reconvene at the end of that time and reconsider our options if there are any problems. But, I have to agree with Mr. Malone. This place has been my home, made me who I am today, and I'm willing to fight to keep the doors open. I'd bet anything that Tessie's energy is just what we need to put a fresh face on the casino." He punctuated that statement with a wink in my direction, and I knew there were going to be more business dinners in our future. Rafe had big plans, and I had a feeling it would be to my benefit—the casino's benefit—if I listened more closely to them next time.

"Let's take a vote," Alfie announced. "All in favor?"

Slowly, one by one, hands timidly slid into the air until the number reached the majority. I couldn't believe it. They voted me in.

Alfie smiled down at me. "Looks like you've got a new job, kid." He paused. "Unless you like selling your arty stuff more?"

I stared at the room full of strangers, some of them smiling at me with assurance, others scoffing, arms folded over their chests. I tried to keep the tone of my voice even as I steeled my spine and said, "I want to do this. For my dad."

Rafe rounded the table and scooped me off my feet, into a bear hug. "That's our girl." He squeezed me even tighter. "I know you can do this," he whispered in my ear.

I felt a shiver ride down my spine at his warm breath tickling over my skin. Part of me was crushed when he let me go. And not just the Teen-me part this time. Damn. I think maybe Adult-me was starting to crush on this guy, too. This could definitely turn dangerous.

Board members shuffled between us, extending their hands to me in good will. I mindlessly shook hands, nodding and smiling at each board member offering their encouragement as I tried to take it all in. I was very glad to see the last person leave the room, finally alone, able to process my thoughts. I sat at the table. The long, polished conference table my dad had manned for years. I stared out at the crystal blue waters, shimmering in the sunlight like they were covered in a fine layer of diamonds. Beyond them the jagged peaks of the snow-dusted mountains reached proudly to the sky, creating a larger than life backdrop. I suddenly had the itch to paint it, to memorialize this moment, this beauty, and this incredible rush of emotions running through me on canvas. It was an itch I hadn't felt in a long time.

And I liked it.

When I finally left the boardroom, I hit the elevator button for the penthouse, the crazy thought that it was now mine just hitting me. Though, truth be told, I wasn't sure Captain Jack and I could fill a place that big on our own. A fact I was sure of as Britton answered the door.

"How do you feel about cats? And roommates?" I asked her.

Her false eyelashes batted at me. "What?"

"Well, I just accepted my father's position on the board."

Britton squealed, grabbing me in a hug to rival a boa constrictor. "Does this mean you're staying?

I nodded. "It also means the penthouse is now mine," I managed to squeak out.

She let go of me, her eyebrows twitching ever so slightly in confusion. "So you're moving in and want me to move somewhere with a roommate and cats?"

I shook my head, a laugh bubbling up in my throat. "No," I said, as I led her to the couch and sat down next to her. "I'm asking if you'd like to share the penthouse with me and my cat."

Her eyes flew open wide, instantly tearing up. "I love cats."

"You can keep the master bedroom. The thought of my dad and you...well, you still have some of your things in there, and most of my stuff is in the other room already."

"Are you sure?"

I stared into her rounded eyes, tears spilling down her face, so much appreciation and honesty in their depths. "I'm positive." Patting her hand, I stood in front of her. "I still have a few things in my suite. I'd better go get them before all of this sinks in, and I pass out."

Britton pounced from the couch, hugging me tightly again. I wrapped my arms around her and returned it as best I could with one bandaged shoulder.

"Thank you, so much," she sputtered through sobs.

Unwinding myself from her arms, I smiled. "I'll be right back."

The trip down to the fifth floor was short. I stood outside the door of my old room, reminding myself that Stintner was now behind bars, and it was safe to go in as I unlocked it. Not that those rational thoughts chased away any of the irrational fear I felt at being back at the scene of my attack. Fear that only increased when I stepped over the threshold and immediately felt the hairs on the back of my neck prickle. Something was wrong. Someone had been in my room again, I could feel it.

I grabbed the nearest item I could find as a weapon...my curling iron off the vanity by the door. I held it out in front of me. I wasn't sure I could do much damage, but they'd be styled perfectly.

"Hello?" I called out. "Anyone in here?" I paused. "Particularly anyone scary?"

Then I rolled my eyes at myself. Like anyone was going to answer. I was being big baby. *Get a grip, girl.* I flipped on the light switch, forcing myself to drop the curling iron.

And then I instantly saw what was different in the room.

The Vermeer.

It was hanging on the far wall of my room, a small, white card tucked in the bottom of the frame.

I took in deep breaths as I approached the priceless piece I had just about given up hope of ever seeing again, almost afraid to touch it as I retrieved the note and read it.

*It's only fitting this painting gets returned to the boss.*
*Alfie.*

The boss. Wow, that was me.

I stared up at the beautiful masterpiece, the careful brushstrokes and shading never ceasing to amaze and inspire me. I couldn't wait to hang it back up in the penthouse where it belonged.

Where I belonged.

# ABOUT THE AUTHORS

Gemma Halliday is the *New York Times* and *USA Today* bestselling author of the *High Heels Mysteries*, the *Hollywood Headlines Mysteries,* the *Janie Bond Mysteries,* and the *Deadly Cool* series of young adult books, as well as several other works. Gemma's books have received numerous awards, including a Golden Heart, two National Reader's Choice awards and three RITA nominations. She currently lives in the San Francisco Bay Area where she is hard at work on several new projects.

To learn more about Gemma Halliday, visit her online at www.gemmahalliday.com

T. Sue VerSteeg was born and raised in the southeast central region of Iowa in the small town of Grinnell. At the age of 21, she moved her parents and family to the beautiful Ozarks of Missouri where they have since made their homes. She has been blessed with the love of an adoring husband (who is also her soul mate), two wonderful children, the best sister in the world and truly amazing parents. Writing has always been a passion in her life as most family members and friends can attest. Long letters, journals and short stories can be found in nearly every drawer and filing cabinet in her home, along with manuscripts and research documents. Her most sincere wish is that you can find as much enjoyment in reading her stories as she did in the creation of them.

To learn more about T. Sue VerSteeg, visit her online at www.tsueversteeg.com

Made in the USA
Charleston, SC
13 August 2013